Who Are You, Linda Condrick?

ALSO AVAILABLE BY PATRICIA CARLON

Who Are You, Linda Condrick?

Patricia Carlon

CARLON
PATRICIA

First published by Ward Lock and Company, Limited
in Great Britain in 1962.

Copyright © 1962 by Patricia Carlon.

First published in the United States in 2002 by
Soho Press, Inc.
853 Broadway
New York, NY 10003

Library of Congress Cataloging-in-Publication Data

Carlon, Patricia, 1927–
Who are you, Linda Condrick? / Patricia Carlon.
p. cm.
ISBN 1-56947-258-0 (alk. paper)
1. Sheep ranches—Fiction. 2. Australia—Fiction. 3. Invalids—
Fiction. 4. Nurses—Fiction. I. Title.

PR9619.3.C37 W49 2002
823'.914—dc21
2002017562

10 9 8 7 6 5 4 3 2 1

CHAPTER I

A LITTLE curl of flame licked backwards round the blackened bole of a tree, touching the runnels of dried sap that had oozed from it in past agony. The curl faded and died, to be renewed again in the fallen tree branches below. The branches twisted, crackling, then were still as another curl of flame followed the first, was lost and followed by a third and then the belching column of grey smoke and orange-red flame of the main body of fire.

The men on the ridge stood silent, watching, as the rising south wind carried the flames back over the way it had come, to flare for a little and die in the dead blackness it had created in its onslaught of the past day and night.

Someone among the group of scarecrow-like, face-blackened men raised a faint cheer, then coughed as smoke billowed back. Out of the grey-blue cloud of it a voice said, "that's done it". No one answered. They were all too tired, had been too tensed and anxious for too long. Now with the south wind came abrupt relaxation, too sharp, too sudden, so that one or two of the black-streaked, hessian-draped figures began to shiver.

Gregory Forst's red-rimmed grey eyes saw the shiver running down the draggled ranks. He was about to speak, then remained silent as out of the smouldering fire dashed a grey-furred body with a runnel of orange fire down the back of the grey. The kangaroo cleared the margin of fire in three crazed leaps, and was among the farther untouched grass, heading for the valley, when somewhere in the background a rifle cracked. The animal gave one tremendous leap upwards, then fell back. Orange-red flame touched out in the grass, flared and went crazily dancing outwards and forwards, doubling and trebling its strength as it went.

Someone cursed and the ragged line moved. Wetted hessian thumped and thumped again round the margin of fire, beating it into the centre, stilling it.

Gregory stood looking down at the animal's body, hardly conscious of his cousin-in-law's shrill voice in his ear, "That'll be happening over and over and it'll take just one fire to start down there and the wind changing on us again and then . . ."

Gregory looked up, into the round face that held a comically boyish look with its blackened streaks where sweat had run through smuts and dried in the heat of flame. Billy McGuire's sun-bleached, greying hair was blackened too, the usually colourless strip of hair on his jutting brows a surprising point of darkness. Like most of them he had damp hessian draped over his shoulders, damp hessian round his waist. Beneath the absurd skirts it formed, Billy's stick-thin legs finished in huge boots. He looked utterly ridiculous. They all did. Gregory's gaze ran over them, and his mouth twitched. It was always like this, he thought in sudden content. The hard fighting, and the fear and the tension and sometimes the pain when men were caught and burned; then the relaxing, the upsurge of talk, the cigarettes passed round—as though they hadn't had enough of smoke!—the looking at one another, and the smiles.

He started to laugh. The sound was taken up. Gazes flicked sideways to companion figures. The laughter grew, above pointed comments on each other's appearance.

Gregory said suddenly, patiently, " Of course there'll be a watch kept, Bill. The fire will go on smouldering for days yet."

Alone of the valley people he called his cousin-in-law Bill—inwardly objecting to the addition to the name that

6

tried to make of the fading, middle-aged man the eternal boy. Yet Billy McGuire *was* a child in some things. Gregory's own patient tone, his explanation where none was due was admission of that. He knew it, frowning at the thought, suddenly impatient both with himself and the man at his side who had fought bushfires every summer, yet must babble as though this were his first.

He was going to say something else when Hudson Forst's voice cracked out further down the line of men. He was standing looking down into the valley, apparently not conscious of his cousin, or of his sister's husband, Billy McGuire.

"Pretty, isn't it?"

His voice touched them all. The tired group turned, slightly or fully as fancy took them, following his gaze. The sun was beginning to wester in red and orange, streaked through with darkened cloud, as though the red, orange and black of the ridge was reflected in the sky, but the light it cast over Leumeah Valley was tawny-gold. Down there in the dusty green of mid-summer things stood out starkly in that tawny-gold light. Sheep that the men knew were dirty grey at close quarters took on an unreal look of white, perfect creatures from story books. Trees were etched in perfection, their faults and blemishes hidden, and the billabong with its drift of weeping willows was silver grey, not mud-choked as it was when you stood beside it.

The red roof of the main two-storeyed homestead was softened to dusky rose, and away beyond it the roofs of the two smaller homesteads were verdant green, while the iron water tanks and the outbuildings were stark white and silver grey.

They stood there, silent, smoking, watching, barely noticing the dust-covered station wagon that had come up the last stretch of the track to a standstill.

"Pretty, isn't it?" the words held them all.

Rowena Searle heard the words as she jumped from the station wagon. She was instantly still, small hands on small-boned hips, her face, with its pointed chin and dark eyes, turning towards the valley, too. She echoed, without turning her head, "Pretty, isn't it?"

The words were echoed again. Mockingly. So that Rowena's dark-brown hair flicked round her face with the sharpness of her turn.

Linda Condrick was almost standing still. But her gaze was on the scarecrow figures of the men, not on the valley. Tall, making the sixteen-year-old at her side appear almost doll-like beside her, she was wearing the crumpled linen slacks and shirt she had worn since she had got up at three a.m. when the moonlight had been a pale-washed reflection of the advancing fire on the ridge.

Dark—so dark that beside Rowena her straight dark hair appeared blue-black and her skin, beside Rowena's golden tan, a shade darker even than olive, she was frowning. The straight, brushed-back hair emphasised the broad fore-head and high cheek-bones, the too wide mouth. She looked almost sullen. Then abruptly she smiled. Linda's smile always startled strangers. Rowena remembered how Gregory had said once, "You're two people, Linda," as though he had suddenly discovered part of her fascination for him. And he had been right. Smiling, Linda's mouth was curved in near beauty to show perfect teeth. Her straight dark brows arched up and the grey eyes became brilliant, the dark-ringed grey irises fully revealed in all their fascinating oddness.

Linda was full of surprises. As now. As she stood looking at the group of men and repeating mockingly, "Pretty, isn't it?" Her gaze still on them she added, "They don't see the ridge any more. Only the valley. I wonder how many of them have turned their backs on past fires, past ruins, past hopes and stared ahead. Is that a bush man's trait, I wonder? To be able to turn instantly away from disaster and only face ahead or . . ."

Then abruptly her smile flashed out. "Don't goggle, Rowena. It doesn't suit you. Do you think they need still more tea? A bath would be more like it, don't you think? Several baths and . . ."

Gregory had turned and was striding down towards them. Linda didn't go to meet him. Just waited. Confident, almost arrogant, Rowena reflected. As confidently, as arrogantly as she had waited, after old Mrs. Forst's death, for Gregory to slip the big emerald on her finger and ask her to be mistress of the Valley.

Gregory's blackened face was split into a smile. Out of the black his red-rimmed eyes had a look only for the girl who waited so calmly, so arrogantly. But just short of her he stopped, laughed huskily as though the smoke was still deep in his throat and said, "I'm filthy, so I shan't come closer. It's licked. For the moment." He looked again towards the valley. "The wind saved us. By not being there at first and then coming over the valley from the south." He asked, "Are you very tired? You went down and rested, didn't you, as I told you to?"

"Yes," the answer came with surprising impatience. Then she smiled, "Yes, I went. Straight after you told me. I've been down at the house ever since. Did you need me?"

"No, Diana coped." His gaze turned again, as though seeking Hudson's sister, Billy's wife, in that crowd of scarecrow figures. "There wasn't any emergency anyway. We've come off lightly this time." His gaze had picked out the woman's figure now and satisfied he nodded, but lifted his voice to call, "Hud—make sure everyone's here, will you?"

That was necessary. Rowena always stood tense through those roll-calls after a fire like this, when black-streaked

A*

scarecrow figures were counted and names were called and answered in hoarse, smoke-dulled voices.

Linda, of course, had never experienced these summer nightmares; never felt the tension, the fear, the sudden rush of sickness in a tensed throat when a voice was slow in answering; never experienced the worse sickness of having a voice, a friend's voice, not answering at all. So perhaps it wasn't surprising she moved slightly away to light a cigarette, apparently absorbed in her view of the valley and not in the roll-call, the counting, the answering, behind her.

Rowena laughed aloud when Hudson's smoke-cracked voice came across, "all here." That was always the same, too. The sudden relief from that nerve-racking tension, the sudden laughter, the abrupt discussion of plans.

Gregory said, "Linda, most of the men will be turning straight home." His gaze went to the line of trucks below them, all pointed towards the valley, all ready to flee across it to the east to the town of Fobb's Creek, carrying the firefighters away in the event of engulfing fire breaking through. "But some had better stay down with us, I think. We can use the shearer's sheds. . . ."

"Of course. It won't take long to put down mattresses and there's plenty to eat."

It was the mistress of the house speaking, Rowena reflected. Not the proposed mistress. But the mistress already, though the wedding wasn't to be for a whole month. There was no trace of the stranger who had come to the valley only four months ago in that confident, "Of course." She might have lived there as long as Rowena herself.

Gregory was looking at her—the stranger, the new-comer, the confident mistress—with an expression that gave no hint he might know how much she was hated by others. He asked with a gentleness that came strangely through the

10

hoarseness of smoke-riddled tones, "You're sure you rested."

"Yes," she said.

And that was a lie, Rowena thought, as she and Linda went back to the station wagon. Linda hadn't rested at all. And surely it wasn't tiredness that had brought that tenseness, that tautness, that restlessness to Linda that afternoon after her abrupt return from the ridge. Usually slow-voiced, almost too sparing of speech, she had talked fast, furiously, almost unceasingly, and often she had gone to the kitchen doorway to stare upwards at the ridge as though it held for her some dreadful fascination of fear.

The men, released from strain for this present moment, were acting like schoolboys. The women watched tolerantly, but alertly. So did Gregory—a different figure now—clean-faced, though still red-rimmed of eyes—with his lean length in clean slacks and white shirt, with his hair washed back to its usual brown. He watched as well, because no one could afford to get drunk, or even half-way to it, tonight. At any minute the alarm might come again and they would have to return to the ridge and a man not sure of his feet, a man too slow of movement, a man with befuddled wits was a danger to himself and to everyone else in the fickle flare and turn of a bushfire. Some of them had seen and all of them had heard, of men who had been slow-witted or slow-footed and found themselves trapped suddenly in a circle of blazing fire, with no way through.

There was to be none of that on the ridge; no disaster for the valley or town if it could be helped. So they watched. Tolerantly, but alertly, and only once had a bottle and glass to be moved out of reach. Out of Billy McGuire's reach. It would be Billy of course, Rowena reflected in nose-wrinkling disgust, then met the gaze—the quick, shame-faced glance round the room—of Diana McGuire, who was obviously looking to see who had noticed her cousin's calm removal of her husband's glass.

Rowena caught the shame-faced glance and tried a re-assuring smile that she realised must have been a failure, because Diana's tired face flushed furiously. A hand reached up nervously to smooth the already too smooth, scraped-back brown hair that finished in a tight little knot at the back of her head. As usual Diana was wearing a washed-out cotton frock. Rowena often wondered where that seemingly inexhaustible supply of washed-out cottons came from. There must be dozens of them in the smaller house at the foot of the ridge, at the northern end of valley, because Rowena never remembered seeing her, except at Hudson's wedding and old Mrs. Forst's funeral, in anything but those washed-out cottons, or faded riding clothes.

Diana crossed to her abruptly, "Where's Wilma? " though she must have known that her daughter was in the kitchen. The big living room led into it and the doors were wide open. Rowena could see Wilma's brown head bent as she worked at slicing bread. She could see, too, the bright, brittle gold of Marcia Forst's hair. Hudson's wife had elected to go home to the other small homestead in the valley and change and come back to this party. She was wearing tight tangerine slacks and a green shirt. Her nails and her mouth would be tangerine, too, Rowena knew. If there was a wrong time for dressing up to the heights of absurdity Marcia would be fated to find it. She was the direct contrast to Diana, which perhaps was why the two women so cordially disliked one another.

Diana was staring into vacancy, her pale mouth slightly open, as though she was groping desperately for something else to say to the girl at her side, when Mrs. Leeming came through from the kitchen. The little sparrow-like figure was as neat as ever, as though there had been no bushfire, no getting out of bed before dawn, no constant invasion of her kitchen, no journey to the ridge with a man's felt hat covering her neat grey hair and a big black apron over her starched white one.

Her little wrinkled hands were folded over the white apron now, her wrinkled cherry of a mouth folded in over toothless gums. She asked, her small shiny eyes on Gregory Forst, "I just wanted to know what I'd better be doing about that tucker for the swaggie. Didn't leave him up on the ridge, did you? "

Gregory frowned. " What swaggie? "

Linda said, " I sent him up the ridge this morning to help out. He came round . . . cadging," her voice flicked her contempt, her disgust of a swaggie's life, " and the Huskin brothers had just called in on their truck. I told him to get up to the ridge and help out and when he came down again there'd be something for him. Not before."

There seemed a sudden deepening of the lines round the man's red-rimmed eyes as he stared blankly.

Hudson's laugh from across the room was mockery, directed at Linda.

" And as soon as you turned your back he'd have nicked out of sight. You should have known that. He's probably ten miles down the track by this."

Linda said coolly, " He didn't. Because I saw the truck start off for the ridge."

Marcia had come to the communicating doorway to listen, leaning there, one hand—tangerine-tipped, Rowena noticed in absurd satisfaction that her guess had been right—on the doorpost. Her small petulant mouth curved in laughter. " And at the foot of the ridge he'd have hopped out, you can bet, claiming falling arches or housemaid's knee! Hud's right. You should have known better."

Linda was still untouched by their mockery, their scorn of

her innocence. Rowena, watching the smoothly expression-less dark face, suddenly wondered if Linda ever really felt, in biting keenness, the dislike of this family she was entering. She went on standing there smoking gracefully, seemingly unmoved as Gregory said, "I'll ring Huskin and make sure."

The room had become suddenly still. They could all hear the lifting of the receiver, of Gregory's voice rising up in question. Then silence and Gregory's voice again. When he came back it was his expression, a greyness of anxiety, that told more than the bald words, "The Huskins took him all the way to the ridge and told him to set-to or walk down again. They didn't see him after that."

"He'da come back, collected his swag and made off to look for tucker somewhere else the men were away fire-fighting," Billy spoke out shrilly through the silence.

"Probably. Did he take his swag with him on the truck, Linda?"

She hesitated, frowning. It was Mrs. Leeming who said, "He left it by the billabong. He asked was that all right and seeing Miss Condrick's a . . . almost a stranger . . . I took it on myself to say it was, providing he left no fire about, but that you'd have the dogs after him if he did."

It was Rowena's eye Gregory caught then. Not Linda's. Not the stranger in the house he looked at to smile in shared memory of times past when a swaggie had come to the door and got the rough side of Mrs. Leeming's tongue. Then their shared smiles died. Because where was the man now? A swaggie didn't pass up the chance of promised tucker unless he was certain of it further on. Even if he had stayed on the ridge, settling down comfortably some-where back of the fire, he would have tumbled out to thumb a lift down in the trucks at the end, to claim he had helped and earned his food. Even if he had come down straight away he would have sheltered under the trees of the billabong and come up when the men returned, to claim the same thing.

Gregory said curtly, "I'll go to the billabong and see if his swag's still there."

"It won't be," Billy burst out. "You know them, Greg. Wouldn't lift a finger if the whole place went. He'da nicked straight back and made off down the road. . . ."

Rowena wasn't listening. She had gone automatically to the kitchen to where the hurricane lamps were huddled, unlighted, on top of one of the cupboards. Her hand reached upwards, reached for matches, lit the lamp while she waited for Linda to come, to take the lamp from her and go with Gregory.

But Linda didn't come. She was still standing motionless, blank-faced, in the living room, when Gregory and Rowena went out, Billy's voice following them, shrilly repeating what he had already said, calling on the others for agreement, a call that sounded as though he was asking more for reassurance than simple agreement.

Outside it was quite dark. Pitch dark at first, because the moon hadn't risen, but when they had crossed the kitchen yard and turned round by the stables and garage there was light—a rose pink haze of glory over the ridge. Rowena could never resist those moments of fascinated pleasure in the rose hazed sky of nights like this, even though the beauty hid a smouldering terror that could, given a change, a rising, of wind, become an engulfing terror.

Gregory abruptly asked, "Did you see that chap up there at any time?"

"What?" Wrenched from her fasinated watching of the ridge, her gaze dropped downwards, to the light from the hurricane lamp in which their shadows danced in monstrous jigging rhythm. "No. I didn't see him anywhere." She gave a sudden giggle and slipped her hand into his. "Anyway, you all looked so awful I wouldn't have known a swaggie from a duke."

He gave a little jerk of laughter, but he said abstractedly, "Linda shouldn't have sent him up. He'd be more likely to find a comfortable spot and go to sleep than to . . ." he stopped.

She shivered against his side. It wasn't a nice picture but it was one that really happened sometimes in these summers of blazing skies and blazing earth; of parched land and dying animals; men sleeping and waking too late to escape the path of onrushing fire.

He asked and his touching hand became a rough grip, "Why didn't you tell her that?"

"I . . . oh, I never saw him at all!" she denied.

"Some of the others—Marcia, Wilma, Diana—must have. And Mrs. Leeming should have said so. But they'd prefer Linda to make her own mistakes, woudn't they? To make herself look a fool."

He glanced down at her and added, "Stop biting your thumb! I thought you'd dropped that habit along with your schoolbooks."

She was glad of the darkness that hid her burning cheeks; but glad of the rebuke that gave her the excuse to ignore what he had said before in such bitterness, and to say instead, "His swag will be gone. What will you bet? Sixpence or the moon?" in the way they had betted jokingly ever since she had come to the valley as a toddler of four —when he had been a tall gangling youth of eighteen, and Wilma had been a bossy, pinafored miss of fourteen.

Rowena was unconscious her thumb had gone back to her mouth, till he struck her hand lightly, jerking her out of memory—of Wilma growing up from pinafores and school tunics to smartly cut riding breeches and lipstick, and laughing glances that were for Gregory alone; to work shared with him and other things shared, too. But it had all fizzled out someway a couple of years ago to the tune of Wilma's angry, impatient cry to old Mrs. Forst, that had been overheard by Rowena, "He doesn't seem to think that a girl he's known all his life has anything left for his finding. He's waiting for someone he thinks it will take a whole lifetime to really know."

Rowena jerked, "sorry", at his rebuking touch, watching the hurricane-lamp light dancing in the fringe of weeping willows by the billabong; dancing through the short-cropped dusty green grass; over the margin of hard-caked mud where the fringe of water had shrunk back with the parching summer; over the water itself, over, finally, the rolled swag and blackened billy, tucked neatly, with a bushman's care, under the protection of two fallen logs.

They stood looking in silence.

Abruptly Rowena held the hurricane lamp high. It shone on Gregory's face, hard and tight and sickened with shock and worry. They were still standing like that when boots crunched over stones and earth to them. Rowena half turned, to see Hudson Forst coming into the edge of the light. He stood shoulder to shoulder with his cousin in height, breadth to breadth with his leanness. They could have been shadows of each other till you looked into their faces and saw that what was all lean strength and determination in Gregory was fast-flabbying softness and indecision in the man who was eleven years older.

Hudson wasn't looking at Rowena or the swag and billy as he stood there, but at the younger man. He said, and his smoke-cracked voice was bitter, "I'll get the men back." He turned on his heel and the heavy boots crunched out four steps away from them. Then he swung round. There was more than bitterness in the crack of his taunting, "Just remember *she* was the fool who caused this!"

CHAPTER II

MAN missing.

Two words repeated over and over through the night. Man missing. Repeated in the scuffle of chairs, the tinkle of telephone bells, the hum of voices over wires. Man missing. Roaring in the start of truck engines; thudding in the tired thump of tired men's feet. Man missing. Flickering in the countless, numberless pricks of light of lamp and torches that danced through the tortured world of the ridge.

As she walked, step by step, in line with Gregory, with Linda, with Hudson, with the others strung out beyond them through the charred monstrous world, Rowena was thinking of Linda's cool, "I did it for the best. All of you were working up there and . . . it seemed indecent he should be shirking and begging food."

There had been only coolness in her voice; only calmness in her face. She had been, as always, in command of whatever emotion was raking her inwardly. Not for her the appeal to others of voice and gesture for understanding; the apology of anxiety. She had waited for the understanding and forgiveness to seek her out, sure it would come, as it had.

Rowena could remember the gentleness of Gregory's answering, "You've not a thing to blame yourself for."

Rowena, feeling the warmth of the ground through even her thick-soled boots, was wondering if that calm mask would crack, even a little, if this man was dead, and if so, what Linda would say. For one moment she felt pity for the woman who walked on her left, then she glanced sideways

18

and saw the dark face reflected in lamp-light and wild resentful dislike went through her at the smoothness of expression.

She wanted to cry into that dark face, " even if you *are* a stranger, and you've never thought of men dying in a bush-fire, surely you feel some anxiety over him? Over those words—man missing? "

She was glad she had to look away, to watch where her feet were treading. Up here the rose red haze of fascination wasn't visible. Instead there was the sullen orange wavering light somewhere down the northern face of the ridge, where the fire was still burning sluggishly back on its tracks, dying in its own shambles of death with the south wind's pressure behind it.

Walking was misery. Boots could slide under fallen branches; crash down as sticks collapsed in a shower of ashes to show sparks of fire among the ash still. Linda commented on that—the only words she had said since they had started out—when she nearly fell over one branch and saw it crumble with the jewel of sparks flickering upwards into the night to fade away into nothing.

For just one moment the mask did crack. It showed in the sickness, the dismay, the panic in her sharp, " Everything's still smouldering underneath. It's monstrous! Like some horrible sore. Like . . ."

Gregory's voice came back to her past Rowena. " That's the trouble. The wind has only to change, flare up the sparks again and carry them down over the ridge to the valley and we'll be in trouble. A lot of this stuff will burn on under the ash for days."

Once or twice they stumbled over the blackened bodies of bush animals. Each time Rowena averted her face. Their section of the searching line was coming to the gully now, she knew. Abruptly she remembered that afternoon and

19

Linda's flight down the lip of it and out of sight. The scene came back vividly as she went on dwelling on it—the dried green of the gully's lip—with the thick haze of clouding smoke in the north spread out as far as the eye could see either east or west—and the gully itself, a depression about four feet deep running from east to west for about two hundred yards. Linda had been running down the lip of it with the gully itself on her left, the smoke on her right—running frantically, her first aid box banging against her hip as she ran. It was so vivid a memory that she was shocked into open-mouthed amazement that the gully and its lip, seen now in lamp-light, was no longer green. The smoke had advanced since that afternoon, with the fire behind it and devoured everything. She stopped, staring at the big dogwood that had once stood there to flower every Springtime. The bole was blackened now, sap-streaked, the sap still wet in places as though the tree was still bleeding in agony. At its foot, stretched stiffly, was the charred body of a big monitor lizard that had crept from its home in a hollow log too late to flee.

The four of them had stopped. Hudson's voice, muted as though the shock of that scene had sickened him too, said, "You know, that gully'd be just the spot a swaggie might choose to use for forty winks. Remember how the fire suddenly got through up here in one roar just about half past four. It'd have been fairly clear up till then. If he'd . . ."

He stopped. No need to go on, and say, "if he'd been having forty winks when the fire reached it he's having a permanent sleep now."

Gregory said curtly, "Stay here with Linda, Rowena. Hud and I will work down the gully and beyond, then come back."

Rowena wanted to protest. Once again she was being the child told to keep out of adult matters; a telling she was finding increasingly galling with her seventeenth birthday only a few weeks away. She stood, kicking angrily at ash, finding fire underneath and watching sparkles of light flash up, while Linda took cigarettes and a lighter from her shirt pocket. The little light showed up the high cheek-bones, the broad forehead, as she leaned her face towards it.

Rowena said, "I'll have one, too." She held out her hand, adding briefly, "Thanks."

But Linda made no move to hand over the cigarettes. The little light remained to gleam on her face as she said, "No. You're better off not starting smoking."

Rowena's hand dropped to her side, then to her other hand, her fingers linking behind her back as she asked quietly, "Linda, don't you ever wonder, just sometimes, that perhaps you don't know, always, what's really best for other people? Sometimes?" Her voice lingered on the word. "I've heard you speaking to Gregory—about Hudson, about Diana and Billy and . . . I've heard your argument. You want them to go and you say it's for their own good, but you're a stranger, a . . ."

The little light went out. Linda's voice came from sheltering darkness to say mockingly, "You heard! One of these days, Rowena, that childish habit of snooping will get you into real trouble. If you try it when you're a nurse you'll get your ears smacked, I assure you. Just as I smacked them once. If you remember?"

Rowena remembered. She could feel again the full humiliation of that day when she had been anxiously listening to the doctor talking of Mrs. Forst's illness to Linda, and Linda suddenly throwing open the door and the sting-ing smack that had followed, across Rowena's left cheek and ear, and the cool, authority of the, "This discussion isn't for your ears, Rowena." She could remember her own whispering, "I've more right than *you* to know how she really is."

The memory hung in her voice as she cried, "I've a right to know what's going to happen to them!" She said rapidly, "That will was all wrong and not fair at all. Mrs. Forst shouldn't have left everything to Gregory—all the valley and *their* homes and their furniture and . . . every whole thing they thought would be theirs. Can't you understand they're frightened, Linda? Because you think . . . it was like when you spoke of the swaggie coming to the door. Cadging, you said, and your voice said what you thought of that. You think they're all cadgers, too, and it's time they all stood on their own feet, but . . ."

"If Mrs. Forst had wanted to make provision for them she would have done so."

"She didn't make provision, as you call it, for me."

"She told Gregory before she died, what she wanted for you. You're young . . ."

"And Hudson's forty—no, forty-one, and Diana's five years older and Billy's five more years on top of that. They're all too old to start again. They expected . . ."

Linda's voice was suddenly savage. "They expected!" she mimicked, "They expected! I know they did. They expected a lot, but now they're going to leave this valley. Oh yes, Rowena, they're going to leave!" Her voice dropped to sudden softness, "Leumeah . . . here I rest . . . that's what it means, doesn't it? Leumeah Valley. . . ."

Rowena could feel little prickles of gooseflesh run over her body in dislike; in something even keener than dislike. It seemed to her as if Linda was saying she had come and seen the valley and decided: Here I rest, and had put down roots, roots that were spreading out and out like some

22

greedy tree, leaving no room for anything or anyone else but herself.

Abruptly torchlight flickered from Linda's hand along the gully. "They're being a long time," her voice was suddenly tighter, faintly anxious.

Jerked from abstraction and that cold dislike, Rowena said abruptly, "Linda, you were up here about . . . half past three, I think? I saw you coming running down the lip of the gully. Did you see the swaggie then?"

The answer was flat, expressionless. "I wasn't near here. Not that I remember."

But she had been. She must have come down from the direction the men were now going. She hadn't come from the north, Rowena reflected. She'd come from the east, running along the gully's lip towards the western end, towards Rowena herself, and had sped past and away. But perhaps she hadn't even noticed the gully, or didn't remember the place?

The shots rang out clearly. Two of them. Close together. Rowena put out her hand to steady herself and gasped, because her clutching fingers touched the still warm, flaking, sap-weeping agonised bole of the dogwood. Sickened, she pulled her hand back and stood there, shivering. In all that world there was nothing to touch but death, because fast on the heels of the two shots down the gully that told all the searchers of man found, came the third shot that called through the dead world, man found—dead.

CHAPTER III

It wasn't just the man they brought back on a stretcher to the homestead, but Marcia Forst, too. In the skin-tight, tangerine pants she had tried to take a long leap, the back seam of her pants had split and she had overbalanced to crash down and injure one knee. The absurdity of the accident and the fleeting grins on tired faces as the story had gone down the line of returning men had taken some of the sting out of the other affair. You could, Rowena reflected as she fetched hot water, liniment and bandages, say in amused exasperation, "Marcia again!" and remember past absurdities that shut out, for a moment's grace, the remembrance of three shots from the gully.

Hudson and Billy had installed Marcia in comfort in one of the low-slung living room chairs. Her embarrassment and fright had gone and now she was enjoying the centre of the stage; the circle of interest; making pained winces as Hudson slit the leg of the tangerine pants and crying out to bring them all to look at the purpling weal of flesh the cut linen revealed.

Wilma McGuire's voice was deep, low, attractive and faintly scornful as she said, "You're lucky it's nothing worse. Why on earth did you join in in those . . . things," her dark glance flicked sudden amusement over the draggled tangerine cloth.

Marcia gave a squeal of pretended horror. "Did you expect me to take them off and go in my knickers?"

Wilma's mouth twitched but she said, "You could have

borrowed something off Linda, as Rowena is even smaller than you are, isn't she? But Linda . . ."

Marcia said lightly, belying the look in her blue eyes as they rested on Linda, "The only thing I'd like to borrow off dear Linda is a pair of her shoes. We all would, wouldn't we? Borrow them and stand in them."

The silence stretched and snapped with the deep voice that asked, "Are you up to answering a few questions, Mrs. Forst?"

It was Mick Gambell's voice, but Rowena didn't look up from her careful walk with liniment bottle and filled basin to where Marcia lay back. Only when she put the basin on the floor did she look up at him—at the man she knew as the cheerful-voiced controller of local football crowds; as the curt-voiced messenger of fire outbreaks; as the exasperated-voiced controller on traffic on show day; as the friendly-voiced visitor to the valley. Now there was a new unknown note in his voice, a new expression in the brown eyes, on the hawk-nosed, darkly tanned face.

He was no longer just Mick Gambell, Rowena realised. He was Sergeant Gambell now. And Marcia, also apparently recognising the note of authority and resenting it, asked in pretended archness, "I don't have to describe my accident, do I?"

He said solemnly, "I just want to know what you can tell me about that chap. What you all can tell me? So if you can tell me now?"

Marcia smiled. "Not a thing. That's all I know."

"But you saw the man when he came to the kitchen door here, didn't you, Mrs. Forst? Did he give you his name? Or say where he'd come from?" He had taken a notebook from his shirt pocket and stood there, rubbing the end of a golden-coloured pencil up and down the ridge of his hawk nose. "We have to put a name to him some way."

Marcia shook her head. She looked suddenly tired and burrowed her head back against the cushions as Rowena started to bathe her injured knee.

"I don't know. I wasn't listening. Tramps give me the creeps if you want to know. It was Linda spoke to him, not me."

Linda was in her favourite pose—leaning against the marbled stone mantelpiece, one arm trailing across it, the fingers of the other holding a cigarette.

She said, "He didn't mention his name. I hardly had any conversation with him at all. He asked for food. I told him to earn it. That was all."

Billy said thickly, throwing the words at her like stones in an effort to disturb her calmness, "Not by a long chalk it isn't all. You sent him up when fool'd've known he'd doss down somewhere. . . ."

The calm went. Linda took three steps forwards, so violently that the greying man stepped backwards away from her sharply, his mouth opening, the lower lip hanging slackly in shocked surprise as she snapped, "You're all going to blame me, aren't you, if you can. This is something the lot of you can throw at me for ever afterwards! I sent a man to his death! A pleasant thought for me to eat with and work with. Is it my fault some lazy, spineless little fool preferred to sleep rather than help the men up there? "

Then so abruptly the change was almost shocking, the smooth mask of control slipped back over her dark face. She took the three steps backwards to the fireplace and leaned on the mantel again, lighting a fresh cigarette, her slim fingers quite steady. She said quietly, "I know you all dislike me, but it's a bit unreasonable, isn't it, to start blaming me for something I couldn't possibly help. I'm sorry, Mick, but I can't help you. I don't know anything about the man and I acted for the best in sending him up to the ridge. That . . ." her grey eyes turned for a moment on Billy, "is all there is to it."

Mick Gambell was looking embarrassed now, Rowena saw in one fleeting upward glance from her job. Yet he must have known of the family's dislike, distrust and fear of Linda Condrick. After all it was quite plain why Mick went to the smaller homestead where the McGuires lived. It wasn't because he wanted to look at Diana's garden or listen to Billy's schemes of what he intended to do—one day. It was because he wanted to marry Wilma and from her he must have learned something at least of the family's horror at Gregory's engagement.

He said, still rubbing down the ridge of his nose with the golden-coloured pencil, "Can anybody add anything to that?" He sounded almost pleading.

There was silence, then a little rising murmur of denial that swelled round the room and finished in silence again as Mrs. Leeming spoke from the doorway into the kitchen.

"His name was Golden. I couldn't put my finger on the word till I saw your pencil. Golden it was."

"Golden?" Mick took the pencil from his nose, held it in front of his brown eyes as though a clue to the dead man lay in its slim length and repeated, "Golden?"

"Golden." The little cherry of a mouth was drawn in against the toothless gums, then relaxed as she nodded, "He was here before once. 'Bout a week before Mrs. Forst died—five weeks back that'd be. I gave him food and he went to the billabong that day, too. He hung about for another day I think then took to the road again without giving us good-day. I knew this morning that I'd seen him before. I couldn't put my mind to his name, not till I saw that pencil. Golden it was. Or so he said it was."

"Golden," Mick repeated.

"Golden." She gave back with a triumphant nod. "Golden."

Rowena wished they would stop repeating it like that. It made the dead man come vividly to life so that she could almost see him—a creature of stubbled chin and stained felt hat with a bobble of corks round the brim; scruffy clothes and whining voice, with a note of bluster in the whine.

In another fleeting upward glance Rowena saw that the big sergeant was still staring blankly at the golden pencil in front of his eyes. He hardly seemed aware that Mrs. Leeming was speaking again.

"It was Miss Condrick who went to the door. 'What're you doing here?' she snaps at him and he gives back in that blustery voice a lot of them use when they know there's no men around to give them short-change, 'Just want to know if there's anything against me camping down there,' and he jerked his thumb down to the water. Miss Condrick said, "No, you don't . . ." but I got in quick and said all right providing he didn't leave no fire about. Best not to be too short with them, as I told her afterwards, and then he asked if maybe she had anything for him as he was clean out of sugar and flour. Right then it was the Huskin men pulled up in their truck and called out to say they were on their way up to the ridge and was there any messages or tucker or stuff to go up? Miss Condrick laughed and said, 'You can take this up,' and nodded to Golden and to him she said, 'If you want anything from me you can ask for it tonight, after you've been up to the ridge helping the firefighters. It'll do you good.' He shuffled a bit and the Huskin men started to laugh. Made him mad I think and he hopped up onto the truck. Sat there like a big crow in the back of it—all dressed in black he was—somebody's funeral clothes likely—

looking at us as the truck started off. 'Be back tonight for what you promised,' he blustered. So I made up a parcel for him. A good big piece of meat and damper and some sugar. When he didn't turn up . . ." she stopped abruptly, biting the word short.

"And now," Linda said, "I'm apparently to get the blame because he's dead."

"What are you talking about?"

Rowena's hand jerked a little over the puffed flesh she was bathing; heard Marcia's inward-breath and said softly, "I'm most frightfully sorry," while her whole mind and thought were concentrated on Gregory.

His eyes seemed sunken deep in the red rims of tiredness and smarting pain. His gaze was fixed on Linda as he stood in the verandah doorway. "Who's blaming you for what happened?" he demanded, and his gaze flicked away and went travelling round the circle of intent faces, meeting eyes.

Rowena watched in dismay. Saw Billy's gaze fall and his feet shuffle; Hudson's gaze travel to the night outside; Diana's gaze slide away to passionate concern in the strip of carpet near her; Wilma's gaze turn kitchenwards; Marcia's gaze drop to intent scrutiny of her knee.

Only Rowena herself managed to hold the gaze for longer than a second and even she finally had to look away. She knew her cheeks were red with temper because she had had to admit that along with all the others she could give Linda no welcome to the place.

She wanted to get up and stamp on the floor in childish rage and storm at him, "Why should I welcome her? After what she said on the ridge? That she intends to have everything."

She looked round at the circle, wondering what they would all say if she told them of Linda's outburst and they were made starkly and definitely aware that there was no charity left to cloak them. Ella Forst's charity had cloaked and clothed and protected them all. They had all expected that charity to continue after her death and grant them the title to their own homes and to security. That was why the brief will had shocked them so horribly with its bald sentences, " all I die possessed . . . my dear grandson, Gregory Howard Forst . . . trusting him to carry out my wishes for the valley."

For the valley.

And all in it . . . those words hadn't been in the will, but all of them had known they were implied. They had all discovered the full humiliation and insecurity of dependence the day the will was read and they had known—all of them, including Rowena herself—that they had stepped from the shadow of Ella's charity to the shadow of Gregory's—a far different, a paler, a smaller, a less protecting shadow by far because it was almost lost in the dominant shadow that was Linda—Linda with her expressed contempt for them all; her hatred of what she called " cadgers "; her slow glances of devouring pleasure as she looked round her at the home and valley that were to her a far different thing from anything she had had before.

Rowena knew quite well that it was the fear of what was going to happen when Linda was finally mistress here that caused the family's strikings-out at Linda, their watchful, finger-twisting, heart-wrenching waiting for Gregory or Linda to come out into the open.

Even Mrs. Leeming knew that fear, Rowena realised, staring at the little wrinkled face that was puckered like a child's in distress as the old woman's gaze dropped from Gregory's, and slid towards Linda and then away.

Mrs. Leeming had got nothing either—after fifty years in the house. She was over seventy now and Rowena was woman enough to know and guess what another woman could do to one she wanted to get rid of—the little insults, the constant pinprickings, the mockery—all weapons to drive out someone who was too old a servant ever to be brutally dismissed.

Gregory said shortly, his circling of them all completed, "No one's blaming you, Linda. They couldn't."

The words held command, warning. They all reacted to it, in resentful tightening of lips; in little straightenings of bodies. But they didn't speak. Whatever their feelings towards Linda, their fear of her, they were afraid to come out into the open in front of Gregory.

Mick Gambell cleared his throat. Heads jerked up again, shoulders moved and straightened. Rowena felt a strange sick withdrawing distaste as she looked at them changing again and realised they were remembering their human dignity; shutting out the fact that they lived here in charity.

The young sergeant said, "I'll have to try to find out where Golden came from. I expect he has relatives somewhere. Most of them do have. Solid, hard-working little people, too."

"The salt of the earth," Linda said dryly, then added, that surprising smile of hers that so changed her crossing her face, "Don't mind me. My nerves are raw." Her glance flickered defiance over the listening circle. She threw her cigarette into the fireplace and dusted her hands together with a gesture of hinting dismissal, "I wish you well with your enquiries, Mick, but I think you have everything from us you can get, haven't you? If so, I think it's time some of us at least got to bed. Is the wind still holding?" She turned to Gregory, and had dismissed all mention of Golden with that question. Had dismissed the policeman's enquiries. Dismissed him too.

Rowena, glancing up, saw the way his brown eyes narrowed and his face darkened. He was resentful and no wonder. He was authority but Linda had coolly taken the reins of authority from him and made nothing of him.

They were all talking fire again. Fire and wind. The latest report from the weather office. That and mention of bringing the sheep in in the morning from the outlying paddocks into the home ones, just in case.

Rowena stood up, her work done, but immediately Marcia's tangerine-tipped fingers started to probe at the bandages.

Rowena said lightly, moving away, " Hello, Mick, remember me? "

He glanced down at her abstractedly, then smiled. " Oh, I hadn't forgotten you."

" Just overlooked me. I'm used to it. I'm just waiting for someone to suggest the infant go to bed."

They drew apart a little from the others and he said, weighing the notebook in his hand thoughtfully, then snapping it shut and putting it back in his pocket, "I hear you're leaving us and the valley soon."

"Yes. I'm going to Sydney. To start training as a nurse. They take you now when you're seventeen, you know, and I'll be that in a few weeks. This last year since school's just been a waiting time."

" A nurse," he said reflectively.

She nodded brightly, "Like Linda."

He asked abruptly, "What's going to happen to everyone, when . . . ? "

"Gregory marries? That's not for me to say, is it? "

"No, it's for Gregory. Or is it Linda who's going to wear the trousers in this household? Why are they so frightened of her? "

"Because . . . she thinks they're charity cases and she doesn't like cadgers and . . . oh, Mick, they are!"

"What you really mean is she's greedy for everything —she doesn't want to share. At least that's what Wilma says."

She suggested, wrinkling her nose at him, "What's Wilma got to worry about? You'll marry her and . . ."

"Will I? Perhaps you could say that about Gregory's wedding? Will it happen? Wilma's hoping it won't." He tapped the bridge of her nose with his pencil and said flatly, "and you're enough of a sticky-break to have realised that's not altogether on account of her parents fears."

She looked down at her hands, pretending absorption in her finger nails. She said, "That was all over—two years ago."

He didn't comment on that—on the romance between Wilma and Gregory that had just fizzled out to nothing. He asked instead, "It's as Wilma says—she asked me if I couldn't make enquires into Linda's past, you know, and I told her it was out of the question—but she's right— what do any of you know about Linda Condrick's past?"

"She's an orphan," her voice chanted softly over the words, "she was brought up by foster parents. Lots of them. One after another. Then she trained as a nurse. She has certificates. She has medals. She has prizes."

"A model of perfection."

She laughed, "And now you sound just like Linda herself at her most mocking!"

"Did old Ella like her?"

"Yes . . . I think so," she said, though she couldn't remember anything Ella Forst had said about Linda except once a cackling peal of laughter as the old lady said, "That girl's an icicle. Wants someone to melt her."

She repeated that now and Mick said shortly, "She was right. All that icy control isn't natural. She seems afraid of ordinary emotions. Possibly that's what's interested Gregory—he wants to know what's underneath."

Then he said, "I shouldn't be talking to you like this." He gave her another tap with the golden pencil. "Stop chewing your thumb and try your nursing skill on Marcia, again."

Rowena looked across and saw in exasperation that Marcia was still pulling at the bandages. She remembered suddenly the time four years ago when old Ella Forst had met her at the station one school holiday to drive her home. Old Ella had never treated her as a child at all, Rowena reflected. She had always been outspoken to her—had been outspoken to her, then. "You'll find few changes, Rowena. Billy is still going to alter the house, as he's been going to do ever since I gave it to Diana; and he's going to write that book he dreams about; Diana's still bickering with him and standing up for him at the same time and Wilma's still the buffer between them. You be careful whom you marry, miss. But Hudson's going to marry. There's a change for you. A city girl with high heels and a voice like a hacksaw." She had laughed as the car had bucketed along the country road at the appalling speed Ella had always driven, "That young lady had better have a child at the double to act as a buffer between her and Hudson—they'll need it before a twelve month's up."

But it was four years now and Hudson and Marcia were still childless and still together. Together, not owning even the table they ate off; together and badly in debt; together and afraid . . . of Linda and her influence, her plans.

Rowena said abruptly, "I've tried to be grateful to Linda, because it's really her doing I'm going to have what Gregory's arranged for me. Mrs. Forst told him what she wanted me to have if she died—an allowance so I shouldn't worry ever about money while I trained, and he was going to give me that month by month only Linda said it would be more generous and better and make me quite independent if everything was all legal now and all settled, so I'm to have two hundred and fifty pounds a year all through my training to add to my hospital salary and then when I'm trained I'll get a thousand pounds . . . outright. It's all going into a long legal settlement and I won't ever have to ask for it or wait for it or . . . it will be there and I'll be quite independent. So I'm trying to feel grateful because . . ."

Mick Gambell said harshly, " You'll never have to ask! No, Rowena, you won't. But you'll never be able to ask either, will you, no matter what happens? Two thousand pounds or about that altogether, won't it be? It sounds generous and it is, but you'll never have need to come back to Leumeah for anything. You'll be independent and Gregory and Linda can forget about you."

Her hand had gone up to cover her mouth. Over it her startled dark eyes met his.

He said grimly, " But two thousand pounds won't be any good to the others, Rowena. It won't buy them a home, or land, and they're too old to train at anything new. I wonder . . ." his gaze went to the girl who stood now with Gregory and Hudson talking of the fire, but he didn't go on to say what he wondered. He caught her hand instead and drew further back, against the hall door. He asked in a lower voice, " Did you go to the billabong any time today? "

" What on earth for? We were rushed off our feet. Why, anyway? "

" What and why . . . your favourite words, aren't they? " He was half smiling at her. " I just wondered if you could say when Golden turned up first. If he left his swag, then

35

came up to the homestead, he could have arrived in the early morning."

She shook her head doubtfully, " What does it matter? " she began, then grimaced as she realised she had asked yet another question and that his smile had broadened. But it went as he said:

" I was wondering if he'd had a chance to poke around the place. The dogs weren't anywhere near the homestead."

" How do you know that? " she asked sharply.

The smile flashed out again. " Because they'd have rushed to investigate a stranger, barking the place down, and you say you never saw Golden at all." The smile became a soft chuckle. " And if you'd heard them barking you'd have had your head out the nearest window crying who, how, why, and what? "

Rowena stood in frowning thought, looking at Marcia's fingers still probing her bandaged knee, but not really seeing the destruction of her neat, careful work. She was thinking of Mick and wondering and puzzling. Abruptly she turned and went out of the room through the hall door and out on to the verandah. The moon had come up and was flooding the world outside and the far corner of the wide verandah, but just by the main steps where the vines clustered thickly over the roof and down the wooden supports, there was only shadow.

Rowena stopped there, because Mick was standing in the moonlight at the far end, one of his big hands behind Wilma's head, tangled in the thick, brown, shoulder-length hair.

He was saying, " I don't know whether I'm being infected by the atmosphere here lately, or whether I'm angry because you're afraid—and you are, aren't you?—but every time I hear something about Linda Condrick I find myself looking two ways at once—one way at the surface value of whatever's she's said or done—and the other digging deeper for hidden motives."

"Have you heard something about her? Something that . . ." she broke off. She said roughly, "That sounded dreadful, didn't it? I didn't know I was capable of such a gloating, hopeful tone of voice. Yes, I'm frightened, Mick. Horribly. And the worst of it is the fright isn't so much of what she might do to us, as what's happening to us. It's as though every greedy feeling in us has got to the top and burst out. At first they just wanted the security of their homes; then it was land as well; then someone suggested . . . I don't remember which one . . . that the whole valley should have been split into three and now . . ." she turned away from him, looking out across the home paddocks, "do you know that now mother and Uncle Hudson are fighting, because she said I should have a share—that the valley should be divided into four—and he tries to shout her down. And then dad claims something is due to him, too, because he's been here so long and he claims old Ella liked him immensely." Her voice sounded choked. "And she didn't. She thought him a fool! And Marcia and Hudson yell him down that their share should be bigger than any mother and Billy get because Marcia is likely to have children—two or three or more and part of the land should be set aside for *that*! Every day it's some horrible new thing someone has thought out. They're fighting and fighting when they've no right to anything at all. What I'm afraid of, too, is that they'll go to Gregory soon and demand what they think is right—they'll play right into that woman's hands, Mick—Gregory will be so disgusted at the greediness, at the demanding, that he'll listen to her then and they'll lose whatever little chance they have of getting anything at all. I think . . . maybe that's what she's waiting for; watching us with those cool eyes and waiting for us to cut our own throats."

She moved her head away from his hand and went to stand a few feet from him, leaning on the verandah railing, "I'm glad, for Rowena's sake, but as you say . . . it could mean Linda never intends her to come back. Perhaps it would be a good thing in a way. We're too isolated for someone her age. I used to feel it, too—you're driven back on yourself for entertainment, or on watching others. She sees too much and hears too much and just at the moment," her voice was suddenly harsh and ugly, "we're neither pretty to look at nor pretty to hear!"

After a moment she went on, "Linda is right, you know. We'd just love to throw this swaggie's death at her for the rest of her days." Then she sighed, "Oh, well . . . it's horrible and she must wish desperately she'd never sent him up, in spite of all that icy calmness. But do you know why we're throwing it at her?" She swung round to face him, "Because we know damn well—Hudson and dad, too—that we other women should have told her he might possibly go to sleep up there and we should warn Greg."

He said mildly, "So everyone is going to blame everyone else and you'll have a field day wallowing in self-pity."

Abruptly she laughed, a soft, warm, quite charming laugh in the moonlight. "Dear Mick. . . ."

"But Hudson won't be thinking of that. Or Gregory. They found him. And they think . . . as I do . . . that Golden didn't die by fire at all."

"Didn't? Do you mean he had a heart attack up there?" Her voice rang out in startled astonishment.

Mick said, "No. He was poisoned."

CHAPTER IV

MICK was saying, "He was lying on his face, you see, and the front of his body was practically untouched by fire. There was a pannikin under him. The fire hadn't reached either and it was half full of something that looked like tea. That was what interested me. After all no one on earth sits drinking tea while a fire roars down on him. If he'd been awake he'd have had time to get out and run. First thing I thought he'd laced the drink with enough whisky or something else to knock him right out, so not even advancing smoke would have tickled him awake, poor devil . . ."—he seemed to be speaking more to himself than to Wilma. "It was odd though he hadn't finished it, though it could have been his second or third drink for all I knew. Then I sniffed at it." He finished shortly, "I've smelt something like that before. That was a suicide." Wilma must have made some movement, because he added swiftly, "Oh, no—I think he must have picked up something from somewhere—thought it was his favourite tipple and laced the tea and then . . . but I don't know. I don't even know if I'm right, though Hudson and Gregory agreed they thought I was. We'll know tomorrow when the doctor's through."

Rowena was standing still. A tendril of vine was caressing her cheek. When she leaned her head further back she could smell the green liveness about her, so different from the smell of smoke and charred wood that seemed to fill her thoughts as she remembered the gully, suddenly picturing Linda running swiftly down the lip of it, the first aid case banging against her hip. What if Linda, a nurse, had been able to save that man. . . .

She stood listening to Wilma and Mick go away, talking now of things that had no connection with the dead man or anything else but themselves. Then Linda's voice spoke from behind her. Rowena turned quickly, seeing the dark figure standing in the main doorway, silhouetted against the light.

Linda asked, "Are you intending to go to sleep standing up, Rowena?"

"I was thinking. Linda, why were you so . . . worried or something this afternoon? I mean, I saw you running down the lip of the gully and . . ."

A tiny tip of light became a steady glow as Linda raised her cigarette to her lips, drawing on it. For a moment, in the glow, her dark face was faintly visible as she said, "I've told you I don't remember being there," then was shadowed again.

"Well, perhaps not, but you ran down to the trucks then and you jumped into the station wagon and you rushed away without even waiting for me to go back with you when you knew I was supposed to and I had to come back with Marcia instead, and you just . . . you *raced* down the track. I thought for a minute you were going to turn right over, but you didn't and when Marcia and I came back you seemed upset. You talked and talked. . . ."

"I must have caught it from you. Babbling seems to be one of your failings, Rowena. And imagination another. I was in a hurry and I drove quickly. Why imagine all sorts of drama into that?"

The words jerked Rowena's thoughts back to another occasion when that cool, detached voice had accused her of using her imagination. "It seems to be a failing of yours, Rowena, to let your imagination run away with you,"

Linda had said, and had added, "There was no quarrel. Mrs. Forst was calling to me. I was in the bathroom with the water running and she's been so upset today she panicked when I didn't seem to hear her calling. Naturally she raised her voice. . . ."

That had been the day old Ella had died, Rowena remembered.

She said stubbornly, "It wasn't imagination. You *were* upset, Linda."

The tip of the cigarette glowed again, lighting up the dark face for an instant. Then there was shadow. Out of it Linda's voice said abruptly, "It's none of your business, Rowena, but, to stop that imagination of yours working overtime, I drove fast and I talked a lot because . . . I was furiously angry." Her voice deepened a little. "When I saw Gregory with his eyes inflamed, with blisters all over one leg I could . . . I felt sick. And savage. He told me to rest—*me* to rest, when *he* . . . I had to work off my temper and fear for him some way or other." She moved slightly backwards and said with faint impatience, "But probably you don't even understand what I'm talking about."

"Oh, I do. I'm not a child, Linda."

"No, you're not a child." The faint mockery was back in the cool voice. "You're starting to be a nurse and very soon, too, you'll be a lady of independent means."

Independent! It was a nice-sounding word, Rowena reflected, watching the dark face lit up again for another second before returning to shadow. Nice, if you didn't realise that it could mean someone with no ties . . . . someone who would go from the valley and have no excuse to return.

Overwhelming anger burst from her in a shrill, "You're going to break all my ties with the family, aren't you, Linda?"

The smooth voice seemed to mock with the answer, "It will be for your own good, Rowena. Believe me, I know what I'm doing is . . ."

But Rowena had brushed past her, her hands over her ears, anger and hate trembling all through her.

Marcia was still enthroned in her chair. She complained, as soon as Rowena came back to the living-room, "You've put the bandage on far too loosely. Look."

"You've been pulling at it." Rowena knelt, glad there was something to do to still that wild trembling of her hands and body.

Marcia said complacently, "Hud agrees I'm better off here. I can't walk anyway. He's going to carry me upstairs just so soon as Wilma gets back. She's gone over to collect some of my things."

Diana was smoking now, though she rarely smoked at all and had expressed open disapproval of Linda's constant reaching for cigarettes. She looked irritated, her sallow face flushed. Like that, with colour in her cheeks she looked almost pretty, but the curl of her mouth wasn't pretty as she said, "At that rate you won't get to bed till after dawn. If Wilma has to collect all that junk— two different colours of nail varnish," she flung towards Rowena in explanation, "and a mass of goo it seems you can't do without for your face—she'll be half the night."

Marcia said sweetly, "You'd do well with a bit of the same goo for your own face, Diana."

Billy's voice same in shrill roughness from across the room, "One of these days she'll have more bottles of stuff than you can dream about, Marcia."

Hudson grinned, wheeling on the older man to suggest, "Done some good investing lately, Billy? How's the oil stock? Going to do Diana up on the proceeds, are you?

From what I've read of it in the papers I'd have thought it more likely you were just about to paper the living-room walls with the dud shares."

Flaming red rushed into the fair man's sun-reddened skin. Rushed up, too, under Diana's sallow cheeks as she put out a hand as though to press her husband back into his chair, though they were the room apart. For just one fraction of a moment the tension stayed, circling the room, flung from one to another to rebound on themselves and be flung back yet again. Then it was all directed to one point alone.

Linda had come into the room. Rowena felt the sudden stillness and saw the sliding glances that went to the hall door. Linda said, "Why don't you drive Diana straight back, Billy? Hudson could drop Wilma off when she comes back. We might need the cars here tonight, so she couldn't very well take one from here, but . . ."

It was a good suggestion. A sensible one. But it came from Linda. And they rejected it passionately, discovering a dozen reasons why it was ridiculous, unworkable. United in common dislike they were on almost pleasant terms to each other, by the time Wilma came back. Her thick brown hair was windswept and she carrying two cases, burdened down with their weight. She dropped one and pushed the other towards Marcia.

"This is yours, Marcia. I don't know what the other is, but I brought it in anyway. It was in the little runabout."

That had been Ella Forst's car—bought just before her death—and of which the old lady had been tremendously proud. It had remained unused, untouched, during her illness, until the week after her death, when the big emerald had appeared on Linda's left hand. Since then the little blue car had been seen frequently in the district, always with Linda at the wheel.

Wilma explained without apology to Linda, "It was handiest and the petrol's down to nothing in the wagon. Someone had better fill up, in case of emergency. Is it your case, Linda?"

They were all looking at it. At the initials on the corner of it.

Rowena was looking at Linda and wondering if it was imagination or if there was a queer mottled look under the darkness of the olive skin. It was hard to tell.

Certainly Linda's voice was quite calm as she said, "Yes, it's my case." She crossed the room in easy strides, her hand outstretched. "Thank you," she said curtly.

Marcia demanded shrilly, "Where were you off to?"

Linda said, "I hoped, nowhere." Her gaze swept round them and fixed on Gregory, who had just come in. She said, "I packed it when I came back from the ridge. The fire seemed so terrible. I've never in my life seen anything like it. I'm sorry, Gregory, if you're disappointed, but I'm afraid that on the subject of fire I'm a coward."

But even then there was no appeal for understanding in her voice. As always she waited for it to come to her. As always, when the understanding was expected to come from Gregory, it came promptly with his quiet, "No one who was a coward would have stayed on the ridge helping the men, Linda. You did wonders, but you're safest here. Remember the firebreak I told you about." His gaze went to the window as though he could see, out there in the moonlight, the wide cleared stretch of land that encircled the homestead and was kept forever like that, an ugly necessity against fire devouring the homestead. "You'd be safer here than trying to flee through the valley if the fire came down. You've never seen how fire can move— it can suddenly be round in front of you, behind you and everywhere else just when you thought you were safe. Here

44

it will be a case of seeing no flying sparks reach the home-stead itself and that no fire gets back of the break. After all, the place has weathered fifty years of fires."

He had explained all that long ago. Rowena quite clearly remembered the explanation at dinner time one day when Linda had asked why trees weren't planted to take away the stark, barren look near the house. Gregory had explained at length, and surely Linda couldn't have forgotten.

But she was saying, "I forgot everything you told me. But I won't again. I'll unpack this wretched thing after-wards. For the moment, isn't anyone ever going to move to bed?"

The words seemed to release a spring in them all. Hudson bent over Marcia and lifted her and, with Linda going ahead, they went upstairs. The McGuires moved verandah-wards with Gregory. The kitchen lights were already off, which meant Mrs. Leeming had gone to her own room already.

Only Rowena was left in the disordered living-room with its clutter of dirty glasses, its empty bottles and filled ashtrays, its disordered cushions and Linda's case standing near the doorway.

I'll try not to hate her, and I'll unpack that for her, she thought suddenly. The weight of it surprised her. She needed both hands to carry it upstairs, to Linda's room. She could hear Linda and Marcia talking to Hudson in the room further along the landing.

She put the case down on the floor and undid the catches. The lid sprang back and tumbled clothes, packed in what must have been frantic haste, spilled upwards and over the sides. Rowena knelt there, looking at them. Linda couldn't have forgotten about the firebreak, about Gregory's warnings of what flight across the valley might mean in case of fire breaking through. Yet she had packed. Like this. Frantically.

Underneath the top layer of things there was a corner of red leather. Rowena touched it, spilling back the other things in the case, staring at the jewel case that had belonged to Ella Forst.

It was a long minute before Rowena could bring herself to open the case. When she did she knelt, staring, automatically counting, renewing acquaintance with everything under her fascinated gaze. The whole life of old Ella Forst, the whole story of success for the valley of Leumeah, was written in those jewels, Rowena knew. Old Ella had told her the story of each piece so often the girl could recite them without thinking, from the thin circle of gold with one tiny diamond to the beautiful, expensive, perfect double row of pearls.

The little ring was old Ella's engagement ring. Money had been tight then, when old Gregory Forst and his younger brother, Luke, had come sixty years ago and more to pioneer the valley. Luke had gone away in the end, selling out his share to his elder brother, who had dug in his toes with Ella at his side and fought the land and conquered it. The house had gone up and fine diamond ear-rings had swung from old Ella's ears. Prosperity had continued and added a second storey to the house in a country where such houses were rare. It had reached out to Hudson and Diana, left on their own, and brought them to the valley to live. The prosperity had continued right up to the flamboyance of those pearls, old Gregory's last gift to Ella before his death when young Gregory, his grandson, had been fifteen.

Rowena was still staring at the jewels, her face white with shock, when Linda came into the room.

The two of them looked at one another, Rowena with the jewel case held close to her body.

She said, "Ella's jewels."

"Gregory gave them to me. Yesterday." There was sudden mockery in the voice, in the grey, dark-ringed-irised eyes. "You can ask him yourself, if you and the family don't believe me."

Rowena didn't say anything. She simply watched as Linda came across and took the jewel case from her. Linda said then, "They were the first things I thought of when I packed."

Rowena stood up. She said, her gaze on the floor, "I was going to unpack for you."

"There was no need, but thanks just the same. Go to bed, Rowena." Her hand was moving caressingly over the red leather of the jewel case.

Obediently Rowena turned towards the door. Her thoughts were chaotic. That Gregory had given Linda the jewels was true, or Linda would never have said so. But Gregory could never have given Linda the brooch that lay at the bottom of the case. The brooch with the centre ruby and the circle of diamond-studded leaves. That had been lost. That had been the cause of old Ella's upset the day she had died. The cause of her hysterics, of her urging of them to turn the house upside down and find it.

The brooch had never been found, Rowena was sure. They had all looked for it that day, and afterwards, when old Ella was dead and the funeral was over. It hadn't been found and a man had come finally from the insurance company and talked with Gregory a long time. Rowena didn't know what the outcome had been, but nobody had ever mentioned the brooch again.

So what was it doing now, lying in the bottom of the red jewel case that now belonged to Linda Condrick?

CHAPTER V

ROWENA didn't know if any of the others had slept. She herself had dozed and woken and dozed and woken again, and with each waking she had slipped from the bed and listened—to the silent house—and gone to her window and looked from it towards the ridge. The rose-pink haze had always seemed the same—neither less nor more. Just riding there. A reminder of smouldering danger hovering over them all and the valley.

That morning seemed to have two dawns. One in the east of gold and pink, one in the north above the ridge of hazed rose that faded with the daylight and became simply a blue-grey haze hiding the top of the ridge and merging it into the washed-blue of the parched summer sky.

When Rowena came down to the kitchen Gregory had gone. Mrs. Leeming, in tight little sentences, said he and Hudson had gone up to the ridge to inspect it. Later on, if everything seemed all right, they would be down to get on with the ordinary work of the valley.

Rowena asked, picking her words carefully because she didn't know if Mrs. Leeming knew anything of Mick's suspicions, "Is there any more news about that man? That Golden man?"

"No." Mrs. Leeming was thumping down the bread-dough that had been rising near the big range. "And you've no cause to fret. Later on there'll be papers sent to us that spoke to him and we'll go answer questions—inquest they call it—but no papers will come to you,

Rowena." Her gaze was suddenly abstracted as she paused in her work. "I hope there's family. Someone to come and follow the poor soul to the grave."

"Follow him to the grave . . ." Rowena shuddered.

Mrs. Leeming gave a vicious poke at the dough. "There's worse things than following a body to the grave, Rowena. There's digging your own with your own silliness, for one. Digging a hole for yourself to fall in with your back-biting and quarrelling. . . ."

Rowena slipped away. She didn't want to discuss that, or talk of graves either.

When she went out it was to see Mick himself. She knew he must have seen her, but he didn't look at her or make any greeting. He had come on horseback instead of by car, and he was tying the gelding to the stable post, sparing leisurely time to reach in his pocket and extract a cube of sugar, offering it with little murmurs.

As he didn't seem to want to admit she was there she stopped, watching. Finally he turned, brushing his hands together and came towards her, to ask without any greeting, "What did you girls do yesterday when you took the tea and food up to the men on the ridge? You were coming and going all day, weren't you? "

She stared, twiddling a strand of her dark hair round one finger. "We just went up," she said vaguely at last, "and filled billies and grabbed some pannikins and made our way along the lines and said 'here' and men gulped down the tea and tossed the pannikins back and we moved on. It was beastly. Everyone was cranky, and the smoke kept billowing out and making us cough and . . ."

"Ummm? I suppose the billies were left by the trucks too? While you took one down the others would be standing waiting? "

"Yes. Some of the men came down to us. Why? "

"Why, what, who?" he suddenly grinned at her, but there was an abstracted look still in his eyes.

She pulled a face, but clamped her lips shut on further questions, waiting patiently.

He said at last, "Golden could have come down and helped himself, I expect."

"Oh no," she was indignant and amused together, "The men would have seen him or we might have."

"You didn't give him a pannikin? See him and . . ."

Indignation won this time. "Not on your life. If he'd come asking I might have . . . with a dollop of poison in it for . . ." She stopped, her mouth twisting in sick dismay.

"Oh, oh. Who's talked? Not that it matters, Rowena, because you'll have to know, and answer a lot of questions."

"What about?"

"About the tea for one thing. He had to get that from somewhere. And about . . . anything poisonous the poor devil could have picked up."

She sighed. "Start asking," she invited then.

He shook his head. "It's not in my hands, Rowena. There's my ordinary job and the need to keep watch on the fire. . . . I've asked for help and two city policemen are coming. By plane. Be here this afternoon."

He reached out a hand, ruffling her dark hair. "Don't look so worried, Rowena. Just be nice to them and answer their questions and stop chewing your thumb."

She blushed. Linking her hands behind her back she asked, "He really and truly was poisoned, then? You know for sure?"

"For sure, Rowena," he agreed and there was a sudden shadow in his brown eyes and a shadow all through his voice that made her look at him with wonderment.

Marcia was still in bed in the little room, opposite

Rowena's own, when Rowena carried in the lunch tray. Already the room seemed filled with Marcia's personality. There was the cloying scent she affected filling the air, the scatter of beauty bottles on the table, two of the paper-backed love novels she read constantly on the bedside table, and even one of the plump ridiculous cushions from her house, propped on the end of the bed—a black cushion with features fashioned in black and red and a red and white scarf bow on top so that it looked like a black mammy's head.

Marcia's house was filled with cushions as odd—with big golden Chinese faces; curly-topped black faces; fantastic fruit and vegetables that looked so odd against the dark solid furniture that Ella had given Hudson along with the house.

Rowena asked, settling the tray with due regard for the other's injured knee, "What on earth did you get Wilma to drag that up for?"

Marcia giggled. "That's my secret cache, my pet. Throw it over. Look!" She turned it over, pulled back the top-knot of the bow and undid a zip fastener, reaching in her hand and drawing it out to throw a scatter of jewellery over the white quilt. "You wouldn't think of looking in a cushion, would you?" Marcia crowed triumphantly at Rowena's wide eyes. "I got a scare that time a couple of years back when Hud and I went away and the house got broken into—remember?" Her gaze fixed broodingly on the engagement ring, the thick gold bracelet and the sapphire ear-rings. "I've only got a bit and I aim to hold on to it. Not like old Ella with that brooch she lost."

Rowena's hand had been reaching for the teapot. She almost dropped it as she asked sharply: "Marcia, did you ever hear that the brooch was found—later?"

Marcia was bundling the jewellery back into the absurd cushion. "It wasn't found. Don't you remember the insur-

51

ance guy coming? Four hundred pounds it was insured for," she added softly. "Four hundred pounds. Just for one brooch." She closed the fastener and refixed the topknot bow, then patted the cushion complacently. "If you were a thief you'd never think of looking in that, now would you?"

"No. Have you got things hidden in all those other cushions all over the house?"

Marcia said bitterly, "What else have I got to keep hidden, pet? Of course I could always stuff them with fruit salts and Hud's liver pills, couldn't I? That"—she tossed the cushion back to the foot of the bed where it sprawled in absurdity—"is about the total sum of our world's goods—everything we can call our own—fruit salts, liver pills, my bits of jewellery and a couple of dozen nutty cushions." The brittle gold of her hair was fanned out on the pillow as she leaned back. "I know they're nutty and you all think I'm one with them, but I'd go crackers in that house without something I'd put into it myself. Have you ever thought of what it's like to live with charity furniture in a charity house, accepting charity to settle your ever-growing debts? But of course you haven't. This has been your home always and no charity about it."

Rowena said angrily, "If you've felt that way about everything my godmother gave you, why haven't you left?'

"Because Hudson was dead sure he'd get a slice of this damned valley when the old lady died." There were deep lines showing from her nose to mouth that made her look bitter and yet, in some strange way, younger and more defenceless. "He's a charity man. That's the truth. He's been brought up to think there was always more charity coming whenever he wanted it. Oh yes, we got an allowance to go with the house, and what happened to it? Hud spent it. I know Diana says that's my fault, but did she do any

better with hers? Giving it to Billy to throw away on investments that went bung as soon as he looked at them was
just the same as Hud throwing it away on gambling and
anything else he fancied. We haven't got a penny because
Hudson always felt he'd get the final charity of a part of
the valley. And now he's scared. And so am I, but I'll tell
you one thing, we're going to fight. I'm going to get that
woman out of here if it's the last thing I do, and that's final.
I wouldn't believe, if I hadn't seen it, that someone could
just walk in and get that much influence over Greg. What's
the matter with him that he can't see she'd chisel the gold
fillings out of your teeth if she had a chance? She's got to
go and then we can get to work on him and make him see
what's fair. Make him divide the valley up in decent
shares." She straightened. "And he's going to make provision for our kids, too. If he won't there's not going to be
anything for Wilma, and that's flat. There's . . ."

Rowena said, " She's not going away."

The tirade stopped. Marcia looked at her with narrowed
eyes, waiting.

Rowena went on, " She told me so. It's you who're going.
And me, too. We're all going. She said so. On the ridge
last night."

Linda had been summoned to the ridge. One of the
men had crashed through a trap of seemingly solid ground
into a deep depression on the ridge and it was thought his
leg was broken. Linda had taken the station wagon and
Wilma and gone to the ridge where the blue-grey smoke
cloud still could be faintly seen.

Rowena stood by the stables. watching her go, then
turned and saw that everyone in that quiet house had been
watching too. Marcia's face showed for one flicker of a
moment behind the lace curtains upstairs, though half an

53

hour previously she had said her leg was too sore for any movement at all. And Mrs. Leeming was standing in the kitchen doorway, her wrinkled cherry of a mouth drawn in tight. Diana, in faded riding breeches and even more faded shirt, stood on the verandah, watching too and in the nearer home paddock Hudson Forst, on his big roan, turned in the saddle to watch the station wagon go by.

Five people. All watching the new mistress of Leumeah ride away. All of them concealing emotion behind blank expressions, but when Rowena entered the house again she felt the place was different somehow—quiet, freed of warring currents that had been sweeping it ceaselessly for . . . since Ella's death, she thought suddenly.

It all went back to that—this change in the valley and the smooth, ordered life here—all went back to Ella's illness and Linda's coming; Ella's death and Linda's engagement.

Too much had come out of old Ella's illness just when Linda had finished her short term of relieving nursing in the town hospital. Dr. Paul had mentioned her and her certificates and her calm efficiency in the same breath as he had told them Ella would have to have a trained nurse. Rowena remembered in shock had gratefully they had welcomed her.

Rowena could remember, too, the way Linda's gaze, that first day, had run assessingly over the house and its contents as Rowena had shown her round. Assessingly. Judging its worth, with her mouth curved in pleasure. As assessingly as her grey, dark-ringed-irised eyes had looked at Gregory Forst, judging his worth, her own chances, though none of them realised that then.

Rowena, coming inside, stopped and looked round her, trying to put herself in Linda's place, to look at everything in the way Linda must have looked that first day. To someone with no family, with only a background of a long series of foster parents, it must have seemed, Rowena knew, a paradise. This perfect house, its comfortable living, its owner's jewels. . . .

There was suddenly sick panic and fear all through her again as the word flared out in thought, and she remembered again the ruby and diamond brooch in the bottom of the jewel casket—the brooch that had no right in the valley at all if the insurance money—four hundred pounds, Marcia had said in longing—had been paid into the estate.

Rowena wasn't even conscious of sounds outside, of steps, of voices, till Mrs. Leeming said at her elbow, her voice a hiss of warning, "They're here."

"They?"

"The police. City police."

Rowena began, "Gregory . . ."

The grey head was shaken, "They said to get whoever of you was home. That's you and Mrs. Forst and she's in bed." As Rowena began to move away she suddenly asked harshly: "What're they doing here? *Two* of them? And one an Inspector into the bargain. All that. Just for a swaggie's death."

CHAPTER VI

ROWENA moved stiffly, wishing that she had Linda's blankness of expression; Linda's self control. She knew her cheeks were flushed as she went out onto the verandah. The two men were looking at her, and almost certainly they had heard what Mrs. Leeming had said.

"Miss Searle, is it?" That was the tall, thin, dry stick of a man with a long narrow face and thinning grey hair, putting a name to her in a light, colourless voice.

She nodded wordlessly.

He said pleasantly, "I am Inspector Quince, Miss Searle." He gave a short nod to the startlingly fair, ruddy-faced, big-shouldered man at his side, "Sergeant Cherside.'

She murmured something, looking down at the toes of her riding boots, adding quickly, "I expect you want Gregory. He's out bringing the sheep into the home paddocks. Because of the fire, you know. If the wind turns it might get through and race down into the valley."

He said gently, "You've had a lot of worry," and sounded as though he was honestly sorry about it.

"Yes, but the very worst bit was this man . . ." She stopped.

He nodded. "Perhaps you could tell me what you can about things and then we'll see the others? Pity to worry them while they're busy."

She led the way into the living-room and Mrs. Leeming's face whisked from the kitchen doorway, the door slamming shut. Rowena turned in embarrassment to look at the men, but they didn't seem to have noticed. The sergeant had drawn up a chair for her and both of them were waiting for her to be seated first. None of the family treated her with such adult dignity, and unconsciously her back straightened and her chin went up.

Quince said, and she knew then that they *had* heard Mrs. Leeming's harsh enquiry, "This may seem impressive, Miss Searle, but when official enquires are made it's usual to have two policemen—one acting as witness to what is said, for official records."

She nodded gravely, but her thoughts questioned, An Inspector? Two men and one an Inspector? while he began, "You saw this tramp. . . ."

"Oh, but I didn't. Haven't you talked to Mick? Sergeant Gambell, I mean. Because he knows I didn't."

"I wanted to be sure." He smiled at her. To have your statement witnessed," he nodded towards Cherside. Both of them were smiling at her, but her thoughts went on questioning, An Inspector? Two men and one an Inspector?

Quince asked, "Did you see this tramp, Golden, when he was here in the valley before?"

"No, not that I can remember."

"Did anyone mention him that time?"

"Not that I remember."

"So you can't tell me how long he was here?"

Her eyes asked Why, even as memory turned back five weeks, searching. Of course, she thought suddenly, seeing the white uniformed figure walking slowly, gracefully, from the house, the breeze gently moving the stiff white veil that hid the dark hair.

"Linda would probably know," she said triumphantly. "If it's important." Her tone expressed doubt. "Because you see she was nursing my godmother, only every day she went out in the afternoon while Mrs. Forst was asleep and

walked for a while and she always went down to the billabong, so I guess she might have noticed when he came and
when he went, though she wouldn't bother speaking to
him, of course."

"No?"

She said in sudden dullness, "Linda loathes that sort of
person."

"Lots of people do. It was Miss Condrick, wasn't it, who
sent him to the ridge, because she thought a little work
would do him good?"

"Yes."

"Miss Condrick went up later?"

"Yes. She was up there ages. Being a nurse, you see,
she was handy in case of trouble. Only Gregory sent her
down in the end because she'd been up there since about
ten or so. She came down . . . some time after half past
three it would be." She was lost again in the memory of
that flying figure rushing down the gully's lip and down
to the station wagon and away. Abruptly she demanded,
"What I want to know is when did he die?" Then stared at
him with a red tide of colour in her cheeks.

He looked faintly amused. He said, "Oh yes, Gambell
told us you'd have more questions to ask us than we had to
ask you. But I wonder why you want to know that,
Rowena?"

She looked up sharply at the friendly note, the half
amusement, the use of her Christian name. She said, leaning forward earnestly, "Well, why didn't he go for help if
he felt sick? And then if Linda had been there she might
have been able to save him even. . . ."

He shook his head. He said quietly, "There was no
time for him to seek help, Rowena. Don't distress yourself and others by thinking and wondering that if he had
had help he might still be alive. He died very quickly.

58

Possibly before Miss Condrick came down, but even if she had known she couldn't have helped him."

Her mouth rounded. "What ever was it?" she asked.

"Cyanide, Rowena. Something that kills quickly. Do you know if there's anything like that in Leumeah?"

"Cyanide . . . she shrank back a little. She said faintly, "Yes there is. Or there should be." Then she shot at him indignantly, "But everything is properly labelled, I can swear to that, because I did it myself!"

"Yourself?" Both of them were watching her.

In distress she said, "Gregory made me a sort of darkroom. One school holiday. I used to do a lot of photography—tons of it—all the developing and reducing and everything."

Quince raised his eyebrows, "Did your godmother let you use dangerous stuff like that?"

"She warned me. And she trusted me. Honestly, everything *is* labelled. I can show you."

"I'll want you to do that. Do you know exactly how much there is?"

She confessed in embarrassment, "No. But I haven't used the darkroom or anything in it for . . . oh, ages. I was mad on it for a while, but this last year . . . there've been so many other things."

"I understand. Is everything locked up?"

She thought, "Yes, but the key's on a hook behind the door and that's not locked, or I don't think so."

"You're positive you can't remember how much you had?"

She shook her head, then brightened, "But Linda might know. She took some photos of the house when she first came—she said she was going to send them to a friend to show her what a lovely place it was—and she said she could develop them herself, so I showed her the darkroom and left it to her. And nurses," she added triumphantly, "automatically notice the level of contents in things. Linda told me so once and told me to brush up my own memory. I'm going to be a nurse myself, you see."

"You don't know of anything—any solution containing cyanide—there is about the place besides what might be in your darkroom?'

"No. There are stock medicines and so on. Gregory keeps them in a big cupboard. Locked," she finished.

He looked down at the outspread fingers of one hand and said, seemingly to himself, "So I have to ask Miss Condrick about the contents of your darkroom shelves and whether she knows how long Golden was here before and if she spoke to him at all.

She stared, fascinated into stillness by the out-stretched, strong fingers. She felt suddenly terribly frightened. And the sick feeling of fright remained with her, as he said pleasantly, "I think, before seeing round the place, that I had better speak to Mr. Forst—Mr. Gregory Forst, that is. Could you take us to him? We'll go in the car. Just tell Owen where to go."

Owen . . . the startlingly fair man seemed suddenly human, almost friendly, with his name known and used freely to her like that. It was as though the thin dried stick of an Inspector had said to her, "Look, here's Owen Cherside. Quite an ordinary person really. Just a witness to what you say."

A witness. To everything she said. She tried to think back. To remember. And suddenly she was wishing desperately that everything she had said so far had been left unsaid altogether.

The two men took the front seats, after ushering her into the back with pleasant courtesy. Gregory wasn't where she had expected. She had to give further directions and the car turned again. "Over there?" Cherside said half doubtfully, looking at the thick cloud, that might have been a companion to the one above them on the ridge, though this one lay low to the earth in front of them.

She explained, "That's the dust the sheep're kicking up. They'll be there."

Nearing it the cloud became a thing of bleating petulance, of sudden darts from the dusty fringes of dirty-grey woolly bodies, of startled baaaaaahs. The car stopped and the sheep began to trickle round it on either side, the lean dark forms of two sheep dogs rushing behind them, forming them into a solid mass again behind the car.

Then out of the cloud of dust rode three figures side by side. Silently it seemed, the hoof beats of the horses deadened under the sound of sheep. Rowena stared, fascinated, at the two bigger figures that might have been reflections of each other—dark breeches, open-necked shirts, their faces masked against the dust with handkerchiefs over mouth and nose; felt, broad-brimmed hats thrust down low over foreheads against the blazing sun. Besides them on a smaller, dappled mare, rode a slighter figure, but a reflection of them—breeches, shirt, hidden face and old felt hat.

Rowena heard, even above the bleating, the baaaahs of protest, the sharp shrill barks of the dogs, the Inspector's soft little whistle. She saw his gaze turn towards the other man. Saw their glances cross and hold. The fair man's eyebrows went up in a little question mark, but neither man said anything.

They didn't need to. Rowena could guess what they were thinking—that these figures might be reflections of yesterday's fight on the ridge, when other figures, masked, dehumanised, almost unrecognisable, had moved through another cloud . . . when a man had died.

Two of the figures had stopped. One rode forward, and

a hand pulled down the masking scarf to reveal Hudson's face, surprisingly clean and pink where the scarf had been, and darkly banded with dirt and sweat above it.

"'Day." He stopped by the car, peering down at the men, looking at Rowena with questioning dark eyes.

She said, "Inspector Quince. Sergeant Cherside. From Sydney. They want to see Greg. Inspector, this is Hudson Forst, Gregory's cousin."

The men nodded. None of them spoke until Hudson half turned in the saddle and lifted his voice above the noise of sheep and dogs. "Greg! Police!"

Two words that rang out, seeming to still everything else, then Gregory came cantering over. As Hudson had done, he pulled down the masking handkerchief and said, "Good-day."

"Good afternoon," Quince returned with more formality, his gaze sliding away for a moment, after the third figure that had cantered past, still masked, not looking at the car. Rowena knew it was Diana who hadn't waited. "I wanted to see you, if you can . . ." The Inspector made a little gesture at the sheep.

"Carry on, Hud," Gregory gave a short nod to the other man, who pulled up the handkerchief again and went cantering after Diana. His voice could be heard, muffled but still clearly audible, giving his candid opinion of the sheep's ancestry as he urged them onwards.

Quince grinned, but said with that affable consideration, "I suppose you're tired out."

"Yes," Gregory agreed briefly. He slipped from the saddle and stood waiting till the last of the sheep went by with another of the dogs at their heels. Then he turned back. "What can I do for you?"

Quince got out of the car. He asked, "Just tell me what you know of this Golden."

"Not a thing."

"Never seen him before?"

"I never saw him at all. Until he was dead."

"You didn't come across him on the ridge, while the firefighting was on?"

"If I had," Gregory said with cool detachment, "I'd have used my boot on the seat of his pants."

"Oh?"

"That is, if I'd caught him sleeping somewhere up there or lying back taking it easy, or slinking around seeing what he could get hold of in the way of food."

"You wouldn't consider it likely he helped?"

"No."

"Yet Miss Condrick sent him up?"

"And Grant Huskin took him up," Gregory reminded sharply. "As a joke, meaning to make him walk down, I expect. They wouldn't expect him to stay there. Linda isn't a country girl. Golden is probably the first swaggie she's come across."

Quince stood silent a moment, then began to ask about the tea that had been taken up. Gregory said briefly, "I drank what was given me. Hands reached out and pushed a pannikin into mine. I gulped and tossed it back and got on with the job."

"Could Golden have helped himself? From near the trucks? Or if a billy was put down by one the girls and she moved away from it for a moment?"

"Possibly, but I can't see him going near the trucks. Too much danger the men might see him. And he wouldn't be likely to follow the girls—they were working along the line of men. Still he did get a pannikin somewhere, and either suggestion could be truth."

Abruptly Quince turned to the subject of poison. Rowena was startled, a little shocked, to hear Gregory listing things one by one, even to what was in her dark-room, according to him, without any pause for thought. Then she realised that he had had a long time to think about it—to worry about it—to try and check over the poisons on the place.

"Anything you can pinpoint as missing?"

"No. But I'm certain of one thing. Of course I can't expect you to accept my word just like that, but I'm certain whatever Golden got hold of didn't come from Leumeah. It's quite possible he poked around in the outbuildings—the dogs weren't near the homestead yesterday so wouldn't have chased him off—but in this place everything bears its correct label. It's been a strict rule in the place ever since I can remember—my grandmother used to give us lurid examples of accidents that had been caused on farms by pouring something poisonous into an innocent-looking tin or bottle. You could say"—a faint smile flickered over his tired face—"that we had it beaten into us from an early age—with the strap. No, I'm quite certain that he got nothing from Leumeah—we're too careful."

Quince turned right away from the subject with his abrupt, "Can you tell me who was on the ridge? Where you were? And when?"

"The last two questions are impossible. We were all over the place. As to the other—everyone going up left word at the police station—Mick Gambell will tell you that. Standard procedure with a fire here. Mick keeps the check list and everyone is checked off when we go. Mick came up mid-afternoon and gave me the list."

"Then isn't it surprising that Miss Condrick didn't ring Sergeant Gambell and report sending Golden up with the Huskin men?"

Gregory said sharply, "No. Miss Condrick, as I've said before, hasn't been through a fire. What's routine to us is unknown to her. I don't think anyone mentioned a check list to her anyway. Rowena . . ." he was looking at her in question.

She said slowly, "I don't think anyone did."

"But Mrs. Leeming—your cook—knew?"

"Good lord, yes. She's been in the valley since the house went up—half a century. But she thought Golden would drop off half way or come straight back to the billabong and hide out till evening, when he'd come back and claim he'd helped out as Linda told him to."

"You've asked her about that?"

"It wasn't necessary to ask. She wouldn't have considered it necessary to trouble Mick about a swaggie."

Again the Inspector seemed to be finished. He said almost apologetically, "If I could see Mr. Hudson Forst . . ."

Gregory put his foot in the stirrup, swinging back into the saddle. "I'll send him back to you."

"We'll turn and follow you down," Quince said with that affable consideration, "save him coming back."

The car followed slowly, stopping when Gregory and the big roan became part of the swirling, noisy dust cloud. He went in and was lost, and a second, two seconds, three seconds later Hudson came looming out of the cloud, masked and unrecognisable.

As before he pulled down the protective handkerchief but he didn't slip from the saddle. He sat there rolling a cigarette with neat, quick movements of his stub-fingered hands.

The Inspector's questions were almost the same. So were the answers he got back. Much as though, Rowena thought, Hudson and Gregory had together been over everything and worked out their answers.

No, Hudson denied, he had never seen Golden until the man was dead. Yes, he would have kicked him off the ridge if he come across him, "that type's just a blasted nuisance", he added to that. Like Gregory he went effortlessly through a list of poisons known to be round the homestead. Like Gregory he stoutly denied whatever Golden had taken by mistake could have come from the valley. He didn't know where everybody had been on the ridge. Only when Linda was mentioned did his ready answers falter for the first time. No, he admitted, his tone dragging with reluctance, there was nothing odd in Linda not ringing the police station and reporting sending Golden to the ridge. She wouldn't, he said, have known of the check list, but it was plain to Rowena, and must, she knew, be plain to the police, that he resented this lifting of possible blame from Linda's shoulders.

Quince seemed to believe in abrupt termination of interviews. He said now, "Was that Mrs. Forst with you?"

"My sister—Diana McGuire. I'll send her back."

He wheeled the horse so sharply that it reared, its front legs pawing angrily at the dust-choked air before it went back into the cloud.

Rowena said, "Mrs. Forst is back at the main homestead. She's in bed. She hurt her knee last night."

"I'd heard about that." Abruptly his lean face split into laughter. "Must have been embarrassing."

She felt suddenly that she hated him. And she was afraid of him, because he was seemingly so apologetic for worrying them with his questions about Golden and unlabelled bottles. . . .

She cried, peering up at him, "But we've only to see the bottle! Why don't you show us the bottle? The one that Golden poured the poison from into his tea? Then we could tell you if we ever saw it before."

He was smiling at her. He said, "You do ask some inconvenient questions, don't you . . . Rowena? And the answer is, we can't because we can't find it."

66

CHAPTER VII

"WHAT have you lost?" Diana had asked, riding out of the cloud of dust to join them by the car, and when he had explained she had said dismissingly, "When you find it, it won't have come from Leumeah." She had given him seemingly no help at all before cantering back after the sheep and Quince said, getting back into the car again, "We'll go back to the homestead, Rowena," as though they were going to make a social visit.

Mrs. Leeming didn't intend to make it one, though. She refused to sit down, so the two policemen stood opposite the little straight-backed woman in the kitchen. She stood with her hands folded over her stiffly starched white apron and admitted, "Yes, I went up to the ridge once. As Rowena will tell you"—she looked quickly at the girl and away again—"but I didn't see him and, God forgive me, I didn't think of him neither."

She expressed no surprise when he mentioned poison. She sniffed. "Mr. Gregory told me this morning," she said flatly. "And though it may sound hard, it would be his own fault. Light-fingered. And look what he got for it. Though mind, it's not usual. For them to steal, I'm meaning, because it's remembered and when they tramp that road sometime ahead they'd get the dogs put on them."

Quince looked down at the scrubbed tiles of the floor. He said abruptly, "I'm not quite sure I have the family sorted. Mr. Forst—Mr. Gregory Forst that is—tells me you've been here half a century." He looked up, smiling at her. "Will you tell me about the family?"

She stared at him. Rowena moved. Her eyes asked Why? and Quince shook his head at her with a little grimace.

Mrs. Leeming said coldly, "If you want the beginning —of the valley I'm meaning—there was Gregory and there was Luke. Brothers. Gregory married Ella and afterwards Luke married Faith and went right away. Gregory and Ella had one son, that was James and . . . there was a daughter, but she went away. She died. Unmarried. Anyway Luke's Faith wrote to say he'd gone and she was remarrying—some foreigner who didn't want Hudson and Diana, so Gregory and Ella brought them here to grow up with James. Then James married and had Mr. Gregory. He and his wife drowned one night in a flood and there was just Mr. Gregory left." She brushed a hand over suddenly too bright eyes. "That's all," she finished abruptly.

Quince said, "So she was probably glad when she had the chance of bringing Rowena here to be company for him."

Mrs. Leeming said curtly, "There was Wilma."

"That's right. Evidently the old lady was a charitable soul, though—she took in her niece and nephew and . . ."

Billy McGuire's laughter startled them all. He was standing—had come silently to stand—in the door between kitchen and living-room. He was wearing crumpled khaki shorts that showed his stick-thin legs finishing in earth-stained boots. He was rubbing his face over slowly, rhythmically, with one of the fleecy blue towels old Ella used to keep specially for guests. Rowena noticed that with irritation; noticed the way the blue was streaked through with a grey that showed Billy's wash after returning from the ridge had been a hurried, incomplete thing.

Billy said, leaning against the door jamb, "Too damn right she was charitable. Old Ella to a T. She'd never'a let it be said by anyone that she'd not done her duty by the family! She had a single-track mind, old Ella, and family was the track. She was stuck-up to the sky about the Forst name and she doled out her charity to keep us all here —even Di, because she was a Forst too—because she was afraid if we left we'd disgrace the family or something. Charity! She'd give the family anything, but you ask 'round what'n old flint she was t'outsiders. Never a penny forced out of her she didn't grudge and try t'get back four times over. Time they forced her to give to the social hall they built in Fobb's Creek with the news everyon'd given but her, she gave all right and then demanded a free scat —the best seat—at everything that was ever put on after, because she reckoned what she'd paid out would've bought more than one seat."

Then suddenly he was raging, his face suffused by spite and bitterness. "She was a cheat, old Ella! Even cheated the family in the end. Know what? Well, then . . ."

Suddenly he broke off. For the first time he seemed really aware that the two men were strangers; were police. He gave a high-pitched, nervous laugh. He tried to catch Rowena's eye, to get her to laugh with him, but when he saw her look of cold disgust his body sagged, his lower lip drooping like an embarrassed child's. He said slowly, "Well, that was an eye-opener for you, wasn't it? But it just got my goat . . . you see, we all got cheated. Her will, you know. But you're police, aren't you? Been up to the ridge and was having a wash and saw you coming up. You don't want my opinion'a the old lady." He blinked rapidly. "How'd we get onto the subject anyway? It's this swaggie you're after."

Quince said with an affableness that made exactly nothing of Billy's strange outburst, "That's right, I'd be grateful for any help you can give me, Mr. McGuire."

Billy straightened a little. His fair hair was on end and he looked a figure of absurdity but he answered with an air of pompous dignity that made Rowena feel a wild desire to burst out laughing: "Any help I can give is yours for the asking, Mr . . . er . . . Sergeant?"

"Inspector. Quince. And Sergeant Cherside," Quince nodded to the silent man with the ready notebook and pencil. The witness, Rowena reminded herself.

The questions were exactly the same. Rowena, listening to Billy's too-wordy replies, felt only impatience. Why didn't they, she wondered, go to the ridge and search again to see if that missing bottle was there or not, and then. . . .

She realised Quince was asking a new question—about any workers in the valley. They all rallied—herself and Mrs. Leeming and Billy—to tell there was one man, out on the west boundary doing fence work now; and one on holidays and one that had walked out on them a week before. They managed otherwise except at shearing and, no, there wasn't anyone helping in the homestead.

Billy went off on a wild tangent to talk of wages and the way, so he claimed, no one wanted to work any more. She felt like crying in wild impatience, "You ought to know. You're so lost in dreams you don't know what work is."

Quince didn't lose any of his affable gentleness. He merely turned the talk to suggest that Billy's own daughter was working hard—helping out, wasn't she, Quince suggested, at some accident?

Billy stared, still rubbing at his face that must have been dry for a long time. He said vaguely, "Oh, she came back. All a false alarm'r something."

Quince looked at Rowena and she moved. She said, "I'll find her for you," and went to move past him.

He said, "And would you ask Mrs. Forst if she'd see me in say half an hour? After Miss McGuire and Miss Condrick?"

She had an idea that if she said no he would suggest an hour, and go on suggesting times till he got his own affable, determined way.

Wilma was standing on the landing, staring into space. She said shortly, "I supppose *I'm* wanted now."

"Yes."

"What do they think I can tell them?"

"Oh—just about poisons and . . . did you see Golden on the ridge? Things like that. They seem to be wasting time almost. Why don't they . . . ?"

"Yes . . ." Wilma's tone was shrill, "Why don't they ask important things? Like, who is Linda Condrick? Do you know that up there I pleaded with her—for mother and dad and . . . she told me she's getting everything. She and Gregory decided what they'd give you and . . . they decided about everyone else too. We're all to get out. And all the valley—the whole valley is going to be hers. She said it was something to do with death duties—in case Gregory died. She's worked on him, persuaded him—it's all to be made over to her! Do you know what I wish?" Her eyes were full of tears. "That I had the cold filthy indecency to say there's some connection between her and Golden and that she killed him! Rowena, don't you see how beautifully all that conversation she had with Golden would fit . . . 'I'll come back tonight for what you have for me,' he said. Oh, Rowena, I'm dreadful. I know it and I don't care. I hate her! If only someone saw her in that gully. . . ."

Rowena said, "But she *was*. By the gully," and stopped, because she could see over the landing railing as she moved sharply and Quince was down there, looking at them.

He said affably, "Come down. Both of you."

Rowena felt drained when she slowly went upstairs again.

He had got out of her everything about Linda running down the gully.

"But what's important about it?" she had asked. "She says she wasn't there. And told me all about driving fast. She was angry. And frightened! She didn't see Golden."

She went into Marcia's room to find her removing nail polish, ready to put on another layer—rose pink this time. She looked up. And stared. "What on earth's the matter with you?"

Rowena sank onto the foot of the bed, picking up the absurd black mammy cushion and balancing it on her knee.

"I've been with the police. The police from Sydney. Two of them. One to ask questions. And one to be witness —to everything you say. They're going to see you next. In half an hour or so."

Marcia shuddered. "My pet, if they have that sort of effect on you—and just go and look in the mirror if you don't know what I mean—I'm not having any. Tell them my knee is killing me."

Rowena snapped, "You don't talk with your knees. And your brains aren't down there either."

Marcia giggled, "Honest, you sound the image of old Ella sometimes. What've they been asking you ever?" She suspended operations on her nails to stare curiously.

"Oh, lots of things—and just now, about Linda. It was all Billy's fault. He threw a scene and then I came up-stairs to get Wilma and she was having hysterics or something and blurted out she'd just love to have someone see Linda on the gully right when the swaggie died, so she'd be involved and I said I'd really seen her there . . . and we looked down and and there they were—two of them— and they have to have two to have a witness to prove you really said what the first one says."

72

Marcia blinked in bewilderment, then she jerked forward, "What? Do you mean to say Linda was in the gully when that man died and never said? "

"I didn't say that. I saw her running down the gully and now that awful man says Golden could have been dead by that time—they're not sure when he really died."

"Why didn't you say in the first place you'd seen her there? "

Rowena leaned forward. She said in a low voice, "Do you know what I thought—oh, maybe I was crazy, but it *was* odd, Marcia! She was running so quickly and she looked quite frantic and she jumped into the wagon and completely forgot I was supposed to go down with her, and then when she got back she was . . . she kept looking at the ridge and gabbling away as though she was frantic about something. I asked her and she denied being near the gully and she said the other was all because she was afraid for Gregory, but . . . it didn't seem like Linda."

"It doesn't," Marcia said coldly. "Not a scrap. That whole business of her packed case was funny, you know. . . ."

Rowena brushed that aside. She said quickly, "I thought . . . just for a while, what if she'd come on him and he said he was ill? You know how she always thinks she knows best about everything. What if she told him he wasn't and then he died. She'd have got a horrible shock. I thought, what if that happened and she wasn't game to tell, and she just ran? " She sighed, "You know maybe Linda is right. I've a terrible imagination."

Then abruptly, angrily, she cried, "But Wilma's got a worse one! Do you know that last night Mick said something about looking two ways at once at everything Linda says or does. He can see the obvious, but he keeps looking below the surface for some other reason to what she's doing.

C⁴

And that's us! Look at me! I just couldn't believe what she said without thinking maybe this happened or that happened. And Wilma's the same. She stood there, and that awful Quince heard her, too, and she said how beautifully those words of Golden's fitted in—that bit about him coming back last night for whatever she had for him—if there was some connection between them. And down there, just now, Quince asked what she'd meant and she said quite baldly, 'I meant if he had something on her and expected to be getting something for not letting it out.' And then she added, 'Who is Linda Condrick, anyway?'"

Rowena tossed the cushion aside and stood up. She said, "I feel a million years old and quite . . . slimy. Something horrid anyway. And I was all wet about that idea, because I asked and Golden wouldn't have had time to tell anyone he even felt sick. Quince said so." She asked wearily, "Is there anything I can get you?"

But Marcia didn't answer. She went on staring into space, her mouth open, the rose pink polish on the suspended brush slowly drying and hardening as she remained motionless.

Rowena repeated her question and when there was still no answer she shrugged and moved tiredly to the door.

CHAPTER VIII

Rowena went softly into the bedroom that had been Ella Forst's—where Ella had died such a short time before and so changed all their lives so disastrously. The windows were half open, the curtains moving sluggishly, but the room still held a faintly musty air of disuse and forsakenness. Rowena hardly noticed that. She crossed to the huge fireplace in the far wall and ducked her head under the stone mantel. Ever since they had been children, she and Gregory and Wilma had known that what was spoken in the living-room could be heard up here in old Ella's room, through the connecting chimney, if you bent your head and leaned inside.

It had also sometimes been used to get even for fancied hurts from one to another—two of them down there asking, "Do you know what Wilma did this morning?" And later Ella would say evasively, "A little bird told me, Wilma, that you went swimming in the billabong this morning right after I said no swimming. Well?"

Now Rowena was using it to know what Linda was going to say. What Quince was going to say. Both of them speaking before a witness. When she knelt there, Linda must just have come into the room below, because she was saying, ". . . to ask me?"

Quince answered, "Whatever you can tell me about yesterday and Golden."

There was a little silence, as though Linda was collecting her thoughts, then she said levelly, " It was a little before ten, just before I went to the ridge myself, when Golden came to the door. I would have told him to clear out, but then

Mrs. Leeming suggested it would be acceptable that he stay at the billabong. I was . . . irritated. By his appearance. And the way he almost demanded food. . . ."

"What did he say? Can you remember exactly?"

"Nearly, I think. He stood there and asked first if he could camp by the billabong. When that was settled, he said: 'Is there anything for me? I'm right out of flour and sugar' . . . something like that anyway. He seemed to consider, in spite of the . . . cadging note in his voice, that there *should* be something put into his hands. It flicked me on the raw. Perhaps you won't understand that, but I've always had to fight, work hard, for what I've gained. I've little patience, and no tolerance, I imagine, for those who expect to get a lot for nothing and no effort on their part.

"And just then the Huskin brothers pulled up in their truck. I told Golden if he wanted food he could earn it. I think it was the Huskin brothers laughing . . . Grant Huskin said something about 'trying to think where you'll have a sudden pain?' at Golden . . . that made him jump on the truck. Afterwards I completely forgot him. I finished packing a few things into my first-aid case and then I followed. I remained on the ridge till about four, I think. I'm not positive. I wasn't clock-watching. And I didn't see Golden, or even think of him, until evening."

The soft, cool voice ceased speaking.

Quince said gently, "It's possible Golden was dead by the time you came down. He would have been lying there in the gully . . . when you ran down the lip of it."

Linda's answer came in a jerkier tone: "I don't remember ever being near the gully. Rowena told me she had seen me there, but I don't remember being there."

"You were running. Does that bring the time closer to the place—tell you where you might have been?"

"I'm sorry. No. I do remember vaguely that I finally

76

decided to come back here and I ran down to the station wagon—it was parked near the trucks—jumped in and drove back. I was angry and upset. I'd seen Gregory and he looked terrible, and just before that the fire suddenly burst through at one point. It . . . I've never seen anything like it before. Gregory told me to go and rest, and I told myself I wouldn't. That if he could stay I could, though I was terribly tired and all that smoke had made me feel vaguely ill. I went away. Then I saw the fire again and I thought the men would never win. I drove back. Packed my case. I kept expecting to see the trucks tearing down to us and someone telling us all to get out. I've had no experience of fires like this."

"No, but you've experience of photography, haven't you?"

"Pho . . . what exactly do you mean?" The jerky little start finished in cool smoothness once more.

"You used Rowena Searle's little darkroom to develop some photos you'd taken of the homestead and valley?"

"Why, yes." She sounded half amused. "And I'm not really experienced. The photos weren't much, but the place was so lovely I wanted a friend to see it, and of course there's no place here to develop prints. I did learn a bit about it at one time and I just dredged up that from memory and went to work."

He asked affably, "And can you dredge up from memory how much was in that can labelled cyanide?"

"So . . . ? No, I'm afraid I can't. I'm sorry."

"You came here to nurse Mrs. Forst, didn't you? That was . . ."

"Four months ago. She was very ill."

"She had no other nurse?"

"Oh no."

"But you, of course, had some time to yourself when the family would sit with the old lady?"

"Why yes. Naturally." The cool voice was puzzled now. "You would have gone walking? To the billabong?"

"I often go there."

"So I expect you would have seen Golden camping there when he was here last—about a week before the old lady died, wasn't it?"

The voice was cold, still as the surface of unrippled water, as she answered: "I have no way of telling you about that as I did not know he was here, nor did I ever see him."

Quince asked, almost gently, "Miss Condrick, how was it you came to Fobb's Creek hospital in the first place?"

"Just chance. I had decided to change my job—to go in for private nursing. I saw the advertisement for a relieving sister and thought the country would be pleasant after the city. That was all."

There was sound in the room below. Sounds as though chairs were moving and feet shuffling. Then Quince said, "Thank you very much," with that abruptness he seemed to bring to the close of every interview. "I won't keep you any further. There's no need for you to bother with us— we'll just have to look around and then get away." Steps crossed the floor below, then stopped. Quince said again, "By the way—how did this fire start, do you know? I'm not exactly clear about signposts on the ridge either— that gully, for instance. We—Cherside and I, that is— haven't been up yet."

Linda said, "It started the other side of the ridge—on the northern face. It slopes down to the creek and Gregory says it was the old story probably—some city people having a holiday and a picnic and forgetting to stamp out their cooking fire. What wind there was from the north and the flames went licking up the slope to the top of the ridge. Everything is tinder dry—it's been a bad summer. The

78

fire was out of hand when the alarm sounded and the men went up. The ridge is too long for them to have beaten it by themselves, according to Gregory—they were really just delaying it, hoping the wind would turn, as it did. The gully is just this side of the crown of the ridge. It runs east to west. The fire came a quarter way down the ridge towards us before the wind turned. You'll see that for yourself."

"So you've seen the ridge previously, but you didn't notice it yesterday afternoon? Or realise just where you were running?"

The still, unrippled voice answered, "I did not notice it. I did not notice Golden."

Rowena was still listening, to sounds drawing farther and farther away when the bedroom door opened and Diana came in. Rowena looked round, cheeks flushed, and Diana gave her a exasperated look.

"I thought I heard sounds." Diana abruptly slumped into the big wing-armed chair near the foot of the big bed. "Not that I really blame you." Her tongue flicked over her lips. In a too casual voice she asked, "What did you hear?"

"Just Linda saying she never spoke to Golden or saw him except that once, and she wasn't near the gully that she remembers and that she doesn't remember about the poison in my darkroom. And Diana, what are they interested in that for? Because it couldn't possibly be that. I mean, it was *labelled*—properly. And even if Golden couldn't read he wouldn't just take some away because it smelt nice or something, and anyway it doesn't. It stinks!"

Diana said slowly: "That's right. If it had been in a whiskey bottle though—something with a smell of its own. . . ."

Rowena said shortly: "But that's just what I've told you.

it wasn't." She sighed, "If only he'd come down. . . ."

Diana's mouth curved in a faint smile. "He wanted that promised food. He was waiting for the time when the men went and he could pour ashes on his head and . . . roll in them, too, the filthy old brute! They'd . . . the men . . . would have been too tired to more than jeer by then. He was just waiting and licking his lips over that promised food. . . ."

Rowena said slowly, "Was it really food? I mean, Wilma suggested that he might have been promised . . ."

Diana shook her head. Reluctantly. And her voice dragged further reluctance as she said, "Much as I'd like to believe that Golden had something on our dear Linda that could have queered her pitch for ever here, so that she had to pay him off . . . with money . . . or a little additive in his tea!"—her smile was suddenly ugly—"I can't, I simply couldn't see Linda stealing into your darkroom and stealing. . . ."

"Diana!" Rowena dropped to her knees beside the big chair, "I want to ask something. Please think carefully. Do you remember that lovely brooch of Ella's?"

Diana was frowning. "What about it?"

"It wasn't found, was it?"

"Not that I know of. In fact . . . Gregory mentioned it the other day—something about it was a pity it had gone because it was one of the finest pieces Ella had." She added slowly: "I wondered afterwards . . . that perhaps he's going to give some of Ella's jewellery to Linda."

"He has. Already. Everything. They were in that packed case of hers. I went to unpack for her and I found the case. Everything was in it."

Diana drew in her breath sharply, pressing her hand to her chest as though something was actually paining her. She said, with apparent effort, "All that," and was quiet

80

for an instant before crying, "She's going to get everything! Oh, *why* did Wilma have to ruin things? We thought she'd marry Gregory and now . . . but there still might be a chance if only . . ."

"But she's going to marry Mick!"

"Yes? Then why hasn't he asked her?" Diana had jumped to her feet to stride up and down the big room. "Because he's afraid she'll say no. She's still hoping that maybe Gregory . . . but what's the good? But it's not fair. To give that woman the jewellery—*Ella's* things! If she hadn't come . . ."—the disjointed words came in jerky little breaths—"even if it wasn't Wilma . . . there was you, Rowena. Another couple of years. A year even . . . oh, stop staring like a little idiot! And for God's sake take your thumb out of your mouth! It's a horrible habit. You're not a child, Rowena. Do you realise that old Ella was married when she was only a few months older than you are now? And you're pretty, Rowena. You always have been. Why shouldn't Gregory have thought of marrying you? And then *she* had to come." She swung round, staring at the girl's startled face. "Why not? I think old Ella herself thought of it sometimes. She said to me once, 'I'd love to be able to call her a Forst'. You, Rowena. She was so proud of the family name. And now that woman's going to bear it. Do you realise that? I wonder what old Ella would think of that? She was too proud really. Do you know, Rowena— our father didn't die for a long time after Hudson and I came here. He just walked out on us and our mother and she divorced him. Old Ella would never talk about it, but that's why we came. She was never going to have Forsts brought up in charity homes—or admit a Forst had deserted his children."

She stood silent and still a moment, then returned to her restless pacing, her jerky speech. "You know, I don't think she ever trusted us, Rowena. Hudson and me, I mean. That's why she paid out to keep us here—so we wouldn't leave and maybe disgrace the Forst name. Here we were under her eyes and I remember, once, she said there was a bad streak in the family." She brushed her hand over her eyes, "God, I'm tired." She slumped down into the chair again. "I think that's the final straw. That woman getting the jewellery . . . it's not right. I was Ella's niece, Wilma's her great-niece. . . ."

Rowena moved. She said, "I wanted to tell you. There was an extra piece in the jewel box. The brooch. I saw it."

Diana's whole body jerked. Her head came forward, her intent gaze raking over the girl's slender body. "What are you talking about?"

"That lost brooch. It was in the bottom of the jewel box."

"What did she say about it?" Diana's hand snaked out to close almost viciously over the girl's arm.

"Nothing. I was so shocked I never said a word. And afterwards I thought maybe it was found and Gregory just didn't say because he didn't want the jewels mentioned because he was giving them all to Linda and you'd all be furious if you knew and . . ."

"You little fool! If she knows you saw it . . . and it wasn't found at all! The insurance money is to be paid. I remember now. When it went I thought of her. The stranger in the house. We all did, but then Ella died . . . I forgot it for a while and then . . ." She seemed lost in some furious abstracted thought; then she swung round on her heel and went quickly out of the room.

Rowena ran after her, but Diana didn't stop. She went into Linda's room. When Rowena followed her, to stand in the doorway, Diana said viciously, "Don't just stand there! Help me find the jewel case and see if the brooch is still there. . . ."

CHAPTER IX

WILMA had been ordered to help Marcia downstairs. Marcia half sat, half lay in the long chair where she had been put on her arrival back from the ridge the previous night, and just as then Hudson Forst stood at the back of the chair. Rowena and Wilma sat on her right. On the left Diana and Billy sat together—close together, united against quarrelling, reproaches or anything else.

It was a semi-circle, all turned towards the fireplace, all turned towards the girl who stood with one arm on the mantelpiece of mottled marble, her head thrown back, her grey-irised eyes almost dark, her body taut, but her face expressionless.

Rowena was suddenly reminded of a time twelve months ago when all of them had been hunting down wild pigs and the dogs had flushed a grey kangaroo. A doe. She had bounded away till she had been faced with rock too vast for her leaps. She had tried twice to clear it, then turned and faced them—the semi-circle of dogs and humans; the dogs darting at her, snapping at her. She had stood motionless, head thrown back, great eyes dark, but no trace of fear on the beautifully modelled features.

Just as the dogs had snapped at her, so now the family were snapping at Linda. It wasn't a pretty comparison, but it remained in Rowena's thoughts as Diana threw the brooch onto the floor. In the hot afternoon sunlight the ruby and diamonds and gold glittered like the sparks of the fire of the previous night, when grey ash had crumbled to reveal what was underneath.

Diana said, "Explain that."

"If you can," Marcia added.

"She can't," Billy gloated softly.

"Because it was lost . . . or stolen," Hudson reminded.

"So where did you get it?" Wilma's fierceness was reflected in her small clenched hands, her flushed cheeks.

Rowena shivered, shuffling her chair in a little back, looking from face to face with darting gaze, taking in the waiting smiles, the thrusting faces, the eager eyes; remembering how Diana had rushed through the house like the storm wind, her voice calling them all to the hunt. Billy and Wilma had been in the kitchen and Hudson had been on his way back to the sheep after stopping in at the homestead for a cup of tea. He had turned back at his sister's shrill calling; had listened; and then had turned to the living-room along with Billy and Diana, with Rowena trailing after them, while Wilma was sent to collect the last of the hunters from upstairs.

When Marcia had come down they had explained the position to her in sharp, fierce, triumphant little words. Linda had walked in in the middle of it. She had known at once, even before anyone had said a word to her, that she was on trial for something. Rowena had seen her abruptly recoil from the avid glances that raked over her, then she had stiffened and stood waiting, and finally gone across the room to stand by the fireplace, seemingly at ease, remembering she was mistress of herself, of the house, of all Leumeah.

Rowena guessed that Mrs. Leeming, left out of it, would have heard through the closed door, between living-room and kitchen, some part of those fiercely triumphant words of explanation and that her greying head would be pressed close to the door panels on the other side, listening to the snapping, the snarling.

84

Linda said, "I found it among my things."

There was one moment's blank silence before they were in full cry after her, "Where did you find it? When did you find it? How did you find it? How did it come there? Why didn't you tell us?"

Now memory was clearer to Rowena than ever of that hunt when the grey doe had stood at bay. Then, Rowena remembered, as she was never to forget, one of the dogs had jumped upwards at the creature at bay. The grey body had risen stiffly, supported on the great rigid grey tail and the tiny, seemingly almost useless front paws caught and clasped the attacker while the back legs with their huge claws had jerked up and torn downwards in great bloody strips of flesh. Rowena could feel the remembered sickness come flooding into her mouth now, because, just as the grey doe had struck, so had the girl by the mantelpiece.

She moved. Two steps forwards and, like claws tearing at them, her voice thrashed out into the silence.

"Damn you! The only thing I can't understand is why you've waited, or couldn't you find it again for all your searching? What did you think when you searched my room and you couldn't find it? You had to wait, didn't you? Till it turned up again. I didn't think it would be noticed among the other things in that case and they're mine. Mine, do you understand? They're mine! Every piece in that box. All of you saw, didn't you, the way things were going. Old Mrs. Forst saw it herself and she was glad! Try to prove she wasn't! That she wouldn't have welcomed me as Gregory's wife. Oh yes, I admit that from the first minute here I wanted him and this house and this valley. You don't, or you won't, believe I could love him, and I don't care. You wanted me out of this house—the stranger who'd come and dared to try to alter your plans. You had it all planned that Wilma should be mistress here, hadn't you? That's why she's held Mick Gambell at arm's length for so long. She wanted Gregory. You wanted that. But I never realised how frightened you were till that brooch went and I was accused. Oh yes, she accused me. In private. Which of you went to her and said 'think of the stranger within the gates? Who is Linda Condrick? What do you know of her?' But there was a delay. The doctor came and I had a chance to search my room first. I was suddenly frightened. And I found it, and I hid it. I've waited and waited and watched you all and tried to decide which of you it was. Or was it all of you? And what did you think when it never turned up anywhere in all the house?"

Rowena couldn't stand any more. She couldn't stop remembering that day with the grey doe's triumph as the hunting dogs had cringed, yelping. Memory held her because the half circle was cringing now. Gazes shifted and circled and moved on and stopped, to move on again as though each was seeking from others the answer to the question, "Was it you? Was it you did it? Was it *you*?"

Rowena knew that the suddenness, the completeness, of that attack with its accusations had made them forget —all but herself who stood outside the half circle—that the attacking words needn't be truth at all, but a screen over the truth; attack meeting attack as the best or only defence. Attack had rebounded and for a moment they cringed. Rowena looked up, into Linda's eyes, and for the first time she saw fear in the dark-circled, grey irises.

Then Linda moved back, back to stand with one arm on the marbled mantelpiece, watching them, waiting, prepared for further attack, but there was none. They cringed, eyes shifting restlessly in that eternal question, "Was it *you*?" Rowena, watching, sick at heart, wondered desperately how long it would be before they rallied and

86

the question changed and grew to a surging, furious, attacking, "But was it any of us at all?"

And, after all, Mrs. Leeming could have had no chance to stand with grey head pressed to the white painted panels of the communicating door, because, when the silence grew and stretched, the door opened, and Quince was standing there, looking at them all.

No one moved. They stared, almost sullenly it seemed to Rowena's tired gaze, at the policeman, who was watching them as he said pleasantly, "All here? Except for Mr. Forst . . . or should I call him Mr. Gregory to avoid confusion?"

"Call him the boss," Billy soured suggestively.

Quince didn't take that up. In that affable way he went on, "I won't keep you long. I was going over to see the Huskin brothers, but Mr. Grant Huskin was driving over here and we met down the valley." He looked round as though he expected applause of this convenience of a kindly fate. "So we had our little chat and it made me think of one or two other points on which you might be able to help me."

They weren't looking at him. They were looking at the stocky little bow-legged man who had appeared behind him. Grant Huskin was nervously twisting the brim of his battered felt hat. He was red to the ears and Rowena felt suddenly like bursting into hysterical laughter. Poor Grant! The shyest and most withdrawing of men. Forced to come visiting with a policeman on his tail and then forced, almost certainly, to stand in the kitchen and overhear a ghastly family quarrel.

As though the awareness of Grant being there and of social conventions that must be repaired if that were possible, at once, they all moved. Marcia's smile glittered; Hudson and Billy muttered, "'Day, Grant. How's things?" Diana asked half distractedly: "Will you have a cup of tea,

Grant?" and Wilma said swiftly, "There's beer on the ice if you'd rather, Grant."

Linda moved then. She said with faint mockery in her voice, "Do come in, Mr. Huskin, and sit down. You too, Inspector. What can we do for you? And will you join Mr. Huskin in beer? Or tea?"

"A nice cup of tea would be very welcome," Quince told her pleasantly.

Bill suddenly gave a snuffled snigger of laughter. "Don't you go adding things to it now, Wilma," he admonished his daughter as she moved swiftly kitchenwards. She turned abruptly and threw him a look of anguished contempt before going into the other room and thrusting the door to behind her, shutting the others in together, shutting them in with Quince. And with the sergeant. With the witness, Rowena suddenly thought. The witness who had stood in the kitchen too and could say, "I heard them quarrelling," if he were asked.

She looked sharply away. At Grant. He was red to the ears again and he was still twisting at his hat. She reached over and took it from his fingers. He gave her a relieved smile, then suddenly burst out, "Look, I only came over to say I was sorry about it. This chap, I mean. Bert and me didn't mean to have all this tumbled onto you. Like I told the Inspector here"—he jerked a broad thumb at Quince—"Bert and me got to playing the fool. At the first gate the swaggie yelped, 'I'll hop off here', and Bert put his boot down hard and yelled back, 'No, you don't, cully. To the top, the lady said, and earn your tucker. And the top it is.' He howled like a dingo and cursed us comin' and going, but we never gave him the chance to get down off the truck and he wasn't game to jump. When we got to the ridge he was still cursing. Bert said to him if he didn't want to walk all the way back he'd have to earn a trip down in the trucks

88

by doing what the lady said. It was a fool trick, but we never paid any thought to the notion he'd just doss down somewhere. We were laughing when we headed off into the smoke and that's the last we saw'a him."

Diana said wearily, "It doesn't matter, Grant, so put your mind at rest. If it hadn't happened on the ridge it would have happened by the billabong—whenever he got hold of a cup of tea. He must have picked up something on the way here—you know some of those swaggies will drink the weirdest mixtures. If it . . . whatever he picked up . . . smelt like whiskey or something, that would have done him."

Rowena said clearly, looking at Quince, "Does cyanide smell like whiskey? And who'd put awful stuff like that into a whiskey bottle? And why aren't you looking for the bottle it must have been in? And why . . ."

Quince looked at her. Abruptly she was silent. He said, still in that affable voice, "You shouldn't ask so many questions, Rowena. Sometimes there are only unpleasant answers to them. Like this time. There was nothing in the tea bar tea itself, milk, sugar and poison."

"But that means"—Diana was staring stupidly at the tea tray with the big brown earthenware pot that Wilma had brought in and put down on the centre table—"that . . . it couldn't have been an accident. You couldn't pick up something containing cyanide and think it was something to drink. As . . . as Rowena said—it stinks!"

Quince smiled. He said, and now his very pleasantness was a mockery, because it glossed over fear, "She's right. Of course Golden's sense of smell could have been defective and if his lungs were full of smoke too . . ." he left that suggestion in the air, as frail as smoke itself, and went on, "He might have even taken a big gulp of tea to clear his throat, without even sniffing at it, if it was handed to him."

He said again, gently, "If it was handed to him. By someone coming out of the smoke."

Rowena thought of them in the car. Quince. And his witness. Looking at one another as three figures rode out of a cloud of dust—masked, unrecognisable. Had they been thinking then of someone walking through smoke, masked, gloved; coming from smoke with outstretched hand offering death to a great black crow of a figure rising up from the gully?

Quince said again, "If it was handed to him. Say he was coughing, and someone came and handed him a pannikin of tea and said . . . what would you say?" He looked brightly, pleasantly round the circle of staring faces.

Hudson said quietly, "Here mate, drink up and wash the smoke out."

Quince repeated the words, seeming to roll them around on his tongue as though savouring them, considering them.

Marcia burst out, "I don't understand! No one would poison a swaggie and that's what you're getting at, isn't it? But if that's so . . ." her eyes narrowed, "there were dozens of people . . . all over the ridge and anyway . . ."

Quince turned to Grant Huskin. "How many of the men up there did you tell about Golden?"

"Eh? Well, none of them. Cripes, we had something to think about beside a swaggie!"

"I thought so. And by the way, how many of you men were carrying cyanide in your pockets?"

"Eh?" Grant stared at him, then gave a sudden roar of laughter. "How many of us . . . ?" he spluttered, smacking his hand down on his knee, then suddenly the laughter stopped. His face had gone a sickly white. He said, "None of us, a'course. You don't . . ."

"No, you don't," Quince agreed. "So now we come to bedrock. Men don't carry cyanide in their pockets on the off-chance of meeting someone they dislike in a handy bush-fire. Secondly, no one but you two men, Mrs. Leeming, Miss and Mrs. McGuire, Rowena Searle and Miss Condrick knew the tramp was on the ridge."

Wilma had poured out a cup of tea, had been about to hand it to him. She suddenly slammed the cup back onto the table so that tea slopped over onto the saucer and table-top.

She said savagely, "So you think it was one of us. One of us women! One of us . . . so you'd better not accept tea from our hands!" She stood there a moment, staring at him and then slowly, horribly, her gaze slid away and went slyly slithering towards Linda Condrick.

Quince was saying, "There's always the possibility, of course, that someone could have left some container on one of the trucks when the alarm went, but the argument remains the same. There was nothing to disguise the smell of what it was. Even if Golden's sense of smell had been defective, even if the container had not been labelled, Golden would never have simply poured it into his tea without first suspiciously testing the stuff with a fingertip, say. And finally there is the fact that we can't find any container at all near where Golden died; the fact the pannikin contained nothing but tea, sugar, milk and poison; and that nothing could have been introduced by mistake into one of the billycans of tea, because no one else became ill.

He went on, "I have had Sergeant Gambell checking steadily through the list of men who went up to the ridge yesterday. So far as we know no man left the ridge from the time he arrived until the wind turned, and no one saw any-one but you girls leaving. None of you have reported a man coming down to the homestead; a man who knew of

Rowena's darkroom and what was in it. And whether or not the cyanide comes from there, the stuff in Golden's pannikin of tea is the same."

He looked down at his outspread fingers before his face in that way Rowena had seen before. "The poison came out of Rowena's darkroom and it travelled to the ridge. It was put into a pannikin of tea and Golden died."

Rowena could almost see it—the thin stream of evil thought and action, sliding out from her darkroom door and slithering in evil length across the valley; wriggling up the track, and across the ridge like the shadow of wind-driven clouds; to become a cloud itself; a cloud of smoke, billowing greyly over the ridge and parting, revealing a masked and gloved, a shadow figure, stepping forward to the gully and offering death.

She was so lost in thought that it was only when the silence became a thing of pressing weight on her senses that she looked up and saw them—the family. Their faces were turned. Their eyes were intent. Their expressions asked in horrible entreaty, "Who are you, Linda Condrick? What have you done?"

CHAPTER X

ROWENA wondered if Quince and his witness had had any plan for going far away at all, or whether they had only planned to go a little way and then return, fear unleashed, on those they had lulled into a false sense of security with their affable, quiet questions.

Because now Quince didn't seem in a hurry to go away. He seemed to have a thousand things to do and the first was to look at the billabong, and the second talk to Gregory Forst.

He chose Rowena to take him—first to the billabong and then to lead them—he and his witness, she reminded herself—to Gregory.

But when they stood beside the water he hardly seemed interested in her explanation of where the swaggie's things had been. He walked slowly round the place and then came back to her and the light-haired sergeant. "A pity," he said, "that, like the swagman in the song, his ghost can't be heard as you pass the billabong, saying what happened to him."

Rowena shivered. He said apologetically, "I've a macabre sense of humour, Rowena. I'm sorry." But his eyes were watchful, as though he knew she was remembering the rest of the song and wondering who, if anyone, would go waltzing matilda the way the swagman had travelled—into death.

Confused, sickened, she reminded herself, they don't hang you these days. Not even for murder. They just shut you up—for the term of your natural life. But that would be dreadful, too—never to walk freely over the valley again, never to. . . .

Appalled realisation flooded over her of the way her thoughts had gone. It was as though she had echoed Quince in his belief that one of them here—one of the family—was responsible. That one of them would be taken away and never see the valley again.

Tightly, deliberately, as they walked back to the car, she marshalled her thoughts as the dogs had marshalled the sheep, coralled them with control and refused to release them to freedom again.

Gregory was busy. With the help of the dogs he was cutting the sheep out from their too-closely packed quarters in one of the home paddocks, into the larger-spread area of three. Hudson and Diana must have helped him herd them into the first paddock, Rowena knew. Almost certainly Gregory would be wondering why they hadn't come back to finish the job. He was intent on what he was doing, his yells of sudden impatience adding to the general noise.

He didn't appear to see them and Quince turned to say to Rowena, "It's all right. We can wait."

One of the ewes darted from confinement and made tracks for liberty, dashing towards the car with one of the dogs, belly low to the ground, chasing after her, snapping at her heels as she halted in front of the car, to give a long mournful "baaaaah!" before turning obediently and becoming part of the woolly huddle again.

Quince grinned. He said, "She didn't like your face, Owen."

"More likely giving her blunt opinion of your theories," was the swift retort.

Then they both turned. Still smiling. To look at Rowena. As though to share the joke with her, to urge her to laugh. But they weren't really, she knew. She had never felt so

94

frightened as when she met their watchful eyes, over those smiling mouths. This was their way. The hunters way, she knew. To lull people into a sense of false security and then to pounce. These men wanted them all—herself too—off guard to their suddenly pouncing questions; their watchful eyes. They were waiting now for her to say something, she knew.

She said at last, "Frankly I think I agree with the sheep."

Quince asked gravely, "Then what do *you* think happened, Rowena?"

"But . . . I thought it was an accident."

"Oh, it might be. It could be. Perhaps it was, and we'll find out we're wrong," he said lullingly and then pounced on her relaxing mind with, "That wasn't a nice quarrel you were having. Now was it?"

She said shrilly, "It's nothing to do with you!"

"I wouldn't say that. No, I wouldn't say that at all," he said pleasantly. "Mind you, I didn't hear all of it. Nice thick door, that, and I didn't come till things were nicely . . . hotted up, shall we say? Like that fire. All bursting out, ready to gobble things up. It seemed to me you were gobbling up Miss Condrick's reputation. The family think she's a thief, do they, Rowena? And she thinks one of them planted that brooch on her to get her out of the valley? Who's right, Rowena?"

She gulped, "I don't know. It's nothing to do with you!" she repeated. "It's . . . a family thing."

"Ah no. Not theft," he corrected. "And then Miss Condrick really isn't family at all, is she?"

"She . . . she's marrying Gregory. In . . . a month from now."

"Well I hope we've gone away by then," he said.

He looked at her, and then away. As though he knew what was passing through her thoughts. He seemed to be intent on the busy dogs and the masked man on horse-back. Then she realised he was humming something—the lilting tune of *Waltzing Matilda*, but he had changed one word—he was murmuring softly, "*Who'll* come waltzing matilda with me?".

She said sickly, "I think you're horrible. Reminding me that when you go away you hope to take someone with you."

He agreed, "Yes, Rowena and, to make sure I don't make a mistake about the one I tell to pack up and come with me, I want you to tell me without any hesitation or asking yourself, should I say this, or should I say that? Just what happened in the homestead just now."

She told him. She spoke in quick, jerky little sentences that gave no betrayal of her own feelings. When she had finished he nodded.

He asked, "Is there anything more you can tell me about the brooch going missing? What did old Mrs. Forst say, for instance?"

"She had hysterics," she said candidly, "and we had to send for the doctor to quieten her. After that the fuss died down a little and then she . . . died."

"Mmmm. By the way, what was this illness that carried her off? Just old age? She was eighty-eight, wasn't she?"

She looked her surprise that he should have known her godmother's age, but answered, "Yes, but it wasn't just old age. She had . . . infectious jaundice. It's got another name but I've forgotten it. And it made her tired . . . exhausted, you know. Weak. And she had a heart attack after all the excitement and Dr. Paul said she just couldn't rally from it."

"Not surprising. It's a nasty thing—nasty for even young people. It would be serious for an old woman. So you had to have a nurse. And it was Nurse Condrick who turned up. And Nurse Condrick whom Gregory Forst's going to marry. And everyone wanted him to marry Miss McGuire, did they, Rowena?"

She scowled. "Wilma's going to marry Mick Gambell. Once it did look as though . . . but that was ages ago. Two years anyway. It all fizzled out."

He turned right away from that with a quick "Rowena, could that tramp—Golden—have got inside the house?"

She stared. "I doubt it, though . . . yes, I suppose he could have if he wanted. We don't keep a watch on all the windows and doors all the time and anyway nearly everything's left wide open in summer. But why . . ."

"You let *me* ask the questions, Rowena," he suggested in that same affable tone. "Think he could have taken that brooch when he was here before? When did Mrs Forst open the jewel case last before she discovered it was missing? Before Golden was here before? And where was the jewel case kept?"

Her mouth rounded in surprise. She sat for several seconds without speaking, then answered slowly, "No, I don't believe that at all. I don't remember when she opened the jewel case. She was in bed and of course she didn't wear jewellery, and anyway she hardly wore any of the pieces ever and Gregory wanted her to send them to the bank because of that, but she said No, she liked to look at them and touch them and then once she loaned some of the things—the necklace and those lovely ear-rings—to Wilma. It was a ball"—she was lost in memory, her dark eyes clouded. "And she said they were quite safe because they were locked up. And they were." Her gaze sharpened again. "Locked in a drawer in her dressing table in her bedroom and she was in bed there all the time Golden must have been here before and oh, he couldn't possibly . . !"

"It was locked up in a drawer of her dressing table in

her bedroom and she was in bed there all the time," Quince repeated. He was looking at the sergeant. At his witness, Rowena reflected. As though reminding that witness to take careful note of those words. She looked from one to the other, anxiously, then Quince said, "But old ladies sleep a lot—especially sick old ladies. There would be times when anyone in the house could open that locked drawer."

She looked away. She said, "Yes," then added sharply, "but you were asking if *Golden* could have taken it. He couldn't ever have had it at all . . . not unless . . ." she stopped again.

"Not unless someone gave it to him," he suggested gently. "Someone in the house?"

She knew she was shaking. She tried desperately to control it, pressing her hands fiercely together in her lap. She burst out, "But the brooch is back in the house now! Linda has it! So it couldn't ever . . ."

She stopped, because it was obvious. If the brooch had been given to Golden for some reason it was back in the house now, and Golden was dead. And he wouldn't have just given it back, surely. . . .

At last she cried, "But it wouldn't even have been any good to him! He wouldn't have even accepted it from somebody even if . . . I mean, what could he do with it? Can you imagine a man like that walking into . . . oh, a pawnbroker's, say . . . and asking if he could pledge that as security for a loan—a brooch of real rubies and real diamonds and real gold that was worth four hundred pounds? The pawnbroker would call the police. Wouldn't he?" she finished triumphantly.

"Let's hope so." Quince was half smiling. He went on smiling, lulling her, she knew, as he added "but what if someone had pledged it *with* Golden in the first place—as security for his silence until cash could be given him?"

She pressed back against the seat. She stared at him. Then she cried, "But you didn't find money on him, did you? Lots of money? Did you?"

"No, Rowena."

He turned away, calmly ignoring her. Leaving her to think—of a brooch being in the house, of Golden being dead, of a brooch that could have been a pledge against a payment and a payment that could have been, at the end, a quick journey to death and not cash at all.

She thought at last, it's back in the house. If it ever went. And Linda . . . Linda says she had it all the time.

When Gregory came over to them, pulling the masking handkerchief down from his face, it was to say curtly, "Sorry. I saw you but couldn't stop. What is it?"

Rowena wanted to get out. To beg to be taken up in front of him on the horse, as they had so often ridden in the past; beg they ride away together while she tell him everything that had happened.

But the Inspector was saying, "Could you tell me something of a brooch that went missing about the time your grandmother died?"

Gregory's dark brows came together. "Good lord, don't tell me you've come across that? Are you going to tell me it was in Golden's possession?" he asked sharply. "That's . . ."

"Not possible?"

"So far as I can see—no. My grandmother kept her jewellery locked up in her own room. Golden couldn't have set hands on it and at the time I asked was she sure she hadn't dropped it outside before she became ill. She told us she'd opened the case several times since she'd had to take to her bed—the last time about ten days before the day she discovered her loss—and the jewel had been there then. I did have an idea. . . ."

" Yes? "

" That she'd dropped it on the bed and it had caught some way in the bed clothes. We had a woman helping in the homestead at that time—because of the extra work with grandmother ill. If she had found the brooch in bundled up laundry . . . it seemed the only solution to me. I think the insurance people investigated the woman afterwards, but they can't have proved anything. The insurance money was to be paid, I do know. Do you actually mean that you've found it. that . . .? "

" It's turned up."

" Where? "

" In Miss Condrick's possession."

Gregory's expression went quite blank. He sat there, motionless, till the horse tossed its head. Then he moved, flicking the handkerchief from his neck, using it to wipe over his face. It was an effective gesture, Rowena knew, for masking any expression that might get through his control as he said, " Oh, where did she find it? "

" Among her things. Right back at the time it first disappeared. She thought some of the family had put it there to try to get the cry of 'thief' yelled at her and get her thrown out of the valley. She hid it again, on her own account, said nothing even to you for fear you wouldn't believe her, and sat down to watch and try to work out who'd played that trick on her."

Gregory said curtly, " And what has all this got to do with your job? You're investigating Golden's death, aren't you? "

Quince said only, " You didn't see any of the fire-fighters leaving the ridge, did you? "

" I was too busy to look. Why? "

"Because there was nothing in the pannikin but tea, sugar, milk and cyanide. Because you don't generally pop poison in your tea unless you want to join the angels and no one has suggested Golden seemed tired of life—in fact he was looking forward to . . . to what the evening was going to give him." His hand stroked gently over his chin. "And that means someone handed him tea laced with poison. And that means someone had to have poison, and you don't, as I've just explained to your family, carry cyanide around in your pocket. And no one but the Huskins, who told no one, and the women at the homestead—who also say they told no one—knew Golden was up here at all."

There was a long silence. Gregory said quietly at length, "I can see no argument against those conclusions, but I can refuse to admit they're necessarily leading you to the truth. You've got your job to do, of course. So what comes next?"

To someone who didn't know him he might have seemed almost disinterested. To Rowena, who knew him so well, he appeared stunned into that level quietness of voice.

Quince was looking at him. Thoughtfully. Then he said, "Could you come up to the ridge with us and show us exactly where you found Golden? We'll drive you up if you can leave the horse—nice looking mare, isn't she?"

Gregory said in that same expressionless voice, "She's a gelding."

Rowena heard the sergeant's little chuckle; saw Quince's sad grimace and hated them both. She was sure that Quince had known. That again he was lulling them; making himself appear almost a fool; was waiting to pounce on lulled senses again. She moved aside on the back seat and a moment later Gregory, after tying the gelding in the shade of one of the trees, slid in beside her.

CHAPTER XI

On the ridge Quince asked to be shown where the trucks had been parked, then followed the black-charred margin of burnt land for some distance, eyes half closed against the glare, stopping to sniff once or twice as though the smell of the burnt-out world held some clue for himself. They watched him silently till he came back.

"All right, can you show me this gully?" he asked.

"Walk carefully," Gregory advised curtly, "you should have worn boots."

The truth of that was soon obvious as the men's light-soled shoes slid and smashed over the burnt treachery of the place. Rowena, in riding boots, walked more effortlessly, while Gregory, apparently unhampered at all, strode ahead.

There was a strangeness about the whole ridge that had nothing to do with the sight of it, Rowena thought, then realised what it was. Yesterday there had been the crackle of fire in the north, the shouts and sometimes curses of men, a thousand sounds. In previous days there had been the cries of birds, the scurry and rustle of creeping things through undergrowth, the rustle of leaves in summer wind—a thousand sounds again. Now if they paused for an instant a total silence was all over them, around them and beyond them in the smoke-smell of the place.

It had affected the men too. When Quince finally spoke it was in little more than a whisper asking, "Where's the fire?"

Gregory nodded down to his feet. "All that stuff—smouldering away under the ash. That's what the trouble is.

If we get a real wind it will scatter the ash and fan up any smouldering fire there is underneath. It would only need a few sparks falling on unburnt land and we'll be off again."

"Isn't there any way you could get water up to it?"

"It would take a deluge. That's what we're hoping for. Several days of soaking rain. A light fall would be worse than useless—it would merely cake the ash together on top and never get down underneath."

He stopped again and the others followed suit, to have that dead, smoke-laden silence all about them. Gregory broke it with, "There's the gully."

They had to work close to the western end of it before they could see it without hindrance from the stark, blackened trees of the ridge. The four of them paced slowly along the northern lip of it till Gregory nodded downwards. Rowena grimaced. It was quite plain where Golden had been—his body had formed a barrier to the fire—there was a little patch of unburned grass there in the middle of the blackened world.

Quince went down into the gully itself, bending close to the ground, with the sergeant at his heels. The witness to everything seen, Rowena reminded herself again. They moved up and down it and came back, to jump up beside Gregory again. Quince stood dusting his hands together as he said, "Thank you very much," with an affability that seemed to make a mockery of the charred world and that horrible patch of sun-scorched green. "I think I have my bearings now. We'll drive you back."

Gregory said curtly, "If you can do without me I'd like to go down and look at things. There are a few men near the creek and others towards the east, nearer town, keeping a watch on things."

Rowena said sharply, shrilly, "I'll come with you. We can walk back, can't we?"

The pair of them stood in that smoke-laden silence till they heard the car start up. Then Rowena's arms were gripped and she was swung round to face him.

"What's this about the brooch?" he spoke softly, whisperingly, into the deathly silence.

She flung back at him, "Was it fair to give all Ella's jewellery to her? Diana was her niece and Linda . . ."

"Is going to be my wife," he reminded coldly. Then he said again, "Tell me about the brooch. Or don't you know?"

Her gaze slid away from his. She said, "Yes, I know. I know. I found it. I saw it last night in Ella's jewel case. Remember that packed case of Linda's? Well, I took it upstairs for her and started to unpack for her and I saw the jewel box and I opened it. The brooch was on the bottom underneath all the other things. She came in and said you'd given them to her. . . ." She stopped, her eyes asking again about the fairness of what he had done. He just looked back steadily and she went on in sudden impatience and anger, "I thought perhaps you'd found the brooch in the last few days and said nothing because you didn't want the jewellery discussed because . . ."

"They'd all fly out at Linda. And myself."

"So you know. How they hate her! Greg. . . ."

"Do you hate her, too, Rowena?"

She wanted to give a quick denial, but couldn't. A slow reddening of her cheeks betrayed self-disgust. Then she said, "I don't know. I wanted to like her because . . . she was going to be part of Leumeah. And, then, she was the one who urged you to make everything legal for me, so I'd have an allowance and be independent and . . ." She fell silent, thinking again of her talk with Mick and what he had said. She sighed. She said, "I distrust her. . . ."

"Why?"

"Oh, Gregory, there's so much! The brooch for one thing. Where did it come from? Is she really telling the truth about it? And Quince keeps hinting all sorts of things in that horrible smiling way of his. And I'm scared! She says she found the brooch and knew everyone hated her because you were falling in love with her and they . . . she said just what the Inspector told you."

"And can't you believe her? Who does she think responsible? "

"She doesn't know. Oh yes, she might be telling the truth." But she heard in her own voice that note that she had heard in other voices—a dragging reluctance to clear Linda of any possible blame.

"Why were the police interested? Who told them? "

"I asked Diana if the brooch had been found and that I'd seen it and she went . . . half crazy. There was a row." She shivered at the memory of Linda turned attacker—the grey doe striking out. "And the police were listening."

He said harshly, "You might have known Diana would fly off the handle." Then he saw her expression. He reached out a hand and suddenly ruffled her hair. "Oh no, I'm not blaming you, Rowena. But I wish you'd come to me." Then he said heavily, "But no, you wouldn't have, would you? You think, like the others, that I'm being unjust." He fell into frowning abstraction, then said, "But why ask if Golden could have taken the brooch if they heard that quarrel and knew Linda had it. . . ." He stopped. There was suddenly such blazing anger in his face that she took an appalled step backwards. He said, "So that's it. She's the one suspected. The stranger in the house. And everyone of them will press the idea to the limit! Why do they hate her so much? She's never done anything to them."

"It's what she going to do! " she burst out. "Can't you honestly see what you've done? Remember her telling us all how she's had to fight all her life long for everything she ever got and then she said," her voice became as cool as Linda's own, "'There's one person I can't tolerate—those who batten on someone else'." She stopped, then went on, "Maybe she didn't mean to do it, but her eyes went round the whole circle of them. That's when they started getting frightened, I suppose, and weren't they right to? Because you're going to turn them out of Leumeah Valley and make them fend for themselves and . . ."

"And they'd rather I married Wilma and then I'd be honour bound, wouldn't I," he said bitterly, "to support her parents. Then if I support them I'd have to support Hudson and Marcia, wouldn't I? Oh yes, Rowena, I can see that, too. And I could see the end of it too—the snapping at each other to make sure nobody got any more than the others—the constant rows. . . ."

She asked curiously, "Is *that* why you didn't marry Wilma? Why you . . ."

"None of your business, Rowena," he said calmly. He stood looking at her, then said, "And they wouldn't have minded if they could have married me off to you, either. They could have twisted you round their fingers to get their own way with me. They've always used you to get hold of information about each other—'Rowena, try and find out what Auntie gave to Hudson last week, and Rowena, drop a hint to Auntie that Wilma's music fees are due' . . . oh yes, Rowena, they've used you. And if they could have married you off to me they'd have gone on using you—'Rowena, drop a little hint to Gregory that I'm worried about some bills'." He ruffled her hair again. "Grandmother used to say there's a bad streak in the Forsts. Perhaps what she really meant was a weak streak, or perhaps that they marry the wrong sort of person." His voice grew hard again, "You're well rid of us, Rowena."

Then he looked at her expression. "Yes, I said the wrong thing, didn't I? The Forsts marry the wrong sort of person. And you think, like the others, that that's just what I'm going to do, too." He put his hands on her arms, and drew her close to him, "Rowena, has Linda ever done anything to you? Ever hurt you? Ever acted against you?"

She knew her face must have twisted into sullenness. She didn't want to answer. She went dredging through memory while the silence lengthened painfully. Then at last she burst out triumphantly, "She boxed my ears once!"

Gregory gave a shout of laughter. He gave her a little shake, then he said seriously, "Yes, and she was terribly upset afterwards. She came to me, Rowena, and told me what had happened. She caught you snooping, didn't she? And I didn't want you, or the others either, to know how very ill grandmother was. Linda knew that." His voice hardened again. "If they'd heard about it I could just imagine them tramping a path to her bedroom filled with pious hopes and hints about the division of her estate. But, Rowena, answer honestly. Has Linda ever acted against you?"

"She wants me to leave the valley," she said stubbornly.

"For your own good. And I agree with her."

She moved impatiently, "Oh, all right, she hasn't, but . . ."

"Then—look after her for me, Rowena. If the others speak out against her, tell me. And if there's anything about her you don't understand, come to me first. Will you promise me that?"

She said slowly, "I'll look after Linda. I promise . . ." then stopped. The silence around them had gone with the sound of boots crunching over snapping branches. They stood, their heads turned to the west, and Rowena was reminded of the previous evening when Golden hadn't even been a name to them. It wasn't sunset, but close to it and the light was gentler than it had been through the rest of the hot day. But she couldn't look down into the valley and repeat the words "pretty, isn't it?" of yesterday. There was too much hate, too many quarrels, too much fear in the valley now.

It was Sergeant Cherside who was crunching his way back to them. His hair showed startlingly fair against the background of blackened, starkly-branched trees. He said, coming to a panting halt, "It takes more energy to cross that than walk twelve miles on the level. The Inspector decided on having a further look round and sent me back to see if you weren't ready to go down yet."

Gregory said curtly, releasing the girl, "Take Rowena. I'll be some time," and moved to face in the other direction, then stopped and looked back at her.

She said, almost against her will, "I'll take care of her. If I can."

"Delicate, is she?" Owen Cherside asked chattily as the two of them started back across the fire-riddled ground. "Miss Condrick, that is."

She said angrily, "Why act as though you and the Inspector want to be friendly and interested in us just as . . . as ordinary people you've met in an ordinary way. You're not. You know Linda isn't delicate. You know quite well what Gregory meant." She stopped and rounded on him furiously, "And sound carries in this silence a horribly long way. I think you heard most of what we said. I bet just anything the Inspector told you to stay just out of sight and listen to us!"

He said quietly, "When you've got a job to do you do it without thinking of niceties of behaviour."

She stood, starting to nibble on her thumb, then hastily
108

linked her hands behind her back. "*Did* you hear what we said?"

"Most of it."

"Does the Inspector honestly think Linda could have given the brooch to that swaggie for something?"

"Has the Inspector said that?"

"He doesn't say anything outright. He walks round and round a thing and leaves you to say a lot you didn't mean to in the first place and then comes out with an innocent-looking question and when you've answered it you realise there's two answers to it. . . ."

She began to hurry away. He came after her in time to put out a hand to stop her falling over a hidden boulder among the ash. Still holding her, his hand firm but quite gentle on her arm, he asked, "Why did Miss Condrick pack her suitcase and have it in her car ready for flight?"

She opened her mouth. And shut it, remembering that to that question too, there were two answers. Flight because of fire, as Linda said, or flight for another reason.

She said clearly, "She was afraid the fire would rush down into the valley and gobble up the house and everything."

He went on holding her. Quite still. And turned her so she could see into the valley. He said with something mocking in his voice, "With that firebreak round the house it would be the safest spot in the valley. Wouldn't it? Try to cross the valley and fire might cut you off before you got far. I saw a fire once. Travelling across level land. Like the valley." He let her go. He said, pleasantly, "You'll look after Miss Linda Condrick best by answering every question as fully as you can. Just remember that."

Marcia's face thrust forwards from the fading light across the bed. Her voice hissed out, "Does Gregory know about the brooch? And about this afternoon?"

Rowena said shortly, "Yes. Let me have a look at your leg and I'll . . .'

"Did Linda tell him?"

Rowena switched on the bedside lamp, then went across to the windows to pull the blind. She came back and said, "No, I did. And before that the police were questioning him. Asking if Golden could have taken it."

"Golden?" Marcia's small petulant mouth was twisting, writhing. She gave a sudden crow of triumph. "Golden! And she has it now!" Her voice went right down to gentle softness. "She has it back now." Her blue eyes were glowing.

Rowena stared at her in sick distaste. She threw at the smiling mouth and glowing eyes, "Gregory believes her!"

Marcia scorned, "What else would he be likely to say? You don't think he's going to admit he could be a fool, do you, my pet? No, Linda took that brooch. Deliberately stole it."

"But can't you see what a terrible risk that would have been?" Rowena urged desperately. "She must have known godmother wouldn't take a loss like that lightly and just as soon as she opened the jewel case and found it gone she might call the police. And she would have, I bet, only she died that night and . . ."

"Yes, she died." Marcia suddenly laughed. "Wasn't that convenient, Rowena? Ella died, right when she might have called the police. Who might have investigated dear Linda and found . . . Who is Linda?" The question raged remorselessly round the room in unleashed rage, "Who *is* Linda Condrick?"

"Marcia . . ."

"Oh, shut up! I don't believe in coincidences. The brooch is found to be gone and Ella dies. . . ."

"You're a horrible person, Marcia," Rowena said with

cold clearness. "Dr. Paul told us all why Ella died. She was tired out and there'd been all that terrible scene over the brooch and even later on I heard her screaming in panic at Linda and getting upset again. And then she had that heart attack and she was too weak . . ." she suddenly took a frantic step backwards from the writhing-faced figure in the bed.

"She was screaming at Linda that day," the tangerine mouth chattered shrilly. "She was screaming at her. Why was she screaming, Rowena? What did dear Linda do? When the brooch was missing and just before Ella conveniently popped off? What was Ella screaming about, Rowena? I remember now! Wilma heard her, too, and told me about it. I'd forgotten. Screaming, Wilma said. Screaming . . . and you heard too. Two of you to tell the police. . . ."

"Marcia, if you say one word, I'll deny everything," Rowena told her frantically. "I asked Linda at the time and she said it was nothing—she had the water running and . . . you're trying to imagine . . ."

She couldn't go on. Linda's cool voice seemed to be filling the room, "It's your imagination, Rowena. I was in the bathroom with the water running and I suppose Mrs. Forst panicked when I didn't hear her."

Marcia had become quite quiet. Her brittle gold hair was fanned out on the pillow as she pressed back on it. She said shortly, "Don't have hysterics, pet. If you don't want to look facts in the face have a look at my knee instead. Come along."

CHAPTER XII

ROWENA slept. Afterwards it didn't seem possible that she had gone early to bed; left all the fear and suspicion and hate and anxiety and gone quietly to sleep and not woken till dawn. When she went over to the window the ridge stood with no haze—the top a dark line of death against the morning sky.

She showered, put on slacks and shirt and went downstairs, the peace of the night flooding away when she walked into the kitchen.

Mrs. Leeming was at the range stolidly frying bacon. The kitchen table was laid and Mick Gambell and Sergeant Cherside rose from chairs either side of it.

Cherside's " Good morning," was lost in Mick's " 'Day, Rowena." They stood, two big men, one very dark, one startlingly fair; one she knew well and one she didn't know at all. She was afraid of them both.

After a moment she realised why they were standing. She plumped down into a chair and said awkwardly, " Oh, sit down," her cheeks red with embarrassment. Mick gave her a little amused smile that only deepened the red. Mrs. Leeming put a cup of tea in front of her. She looked at it, then glanced up and saw both men were watching her, one in simple watchfulness, the other in earnest sympathy.

Deliberately she forced herself to sugar the tea and sip at it, but the very action made her feel sick; made her remember all over again why Cherside was sitting there in this kitchen.

She said with forced brightness, " You're out early."

"We've a lot to do," Cherside returned pleasantly.

"What?" she jerked.

"Ask questions."

She shook her head impatiently, "We've answered them all a dozen times. We didn't know Golden; we didn't see him on the ridge; we don't . . ."

"This time they'll be about Mrs. Forst's death."

Her hand knocked against the cup and turned it over. Both men were instantly on their feet. Mick, accustomed to the kitchen, grabbed the dishcloth ad started mopping at the tea dripping over the cloth and down the edge of the table, while Owen Cherside pulled out his handkerchief to dab at her slacks where the tea had spilt too.

He looked up at her as he worked as though he expected her to say something, but it was Mrs. Leeming, her hands folded over her stiffly starched white apron, who said aggressively, "What are you meaning?"

"Just that we have to ask questions into Mrs. Forst's death. When there's one death in a place, shortly followed by another . . ." He didn't go on. His gaze went round the room—from Rowena to Mrs. Leeming, and on to Mick Gambell, then back to the girl.

Mrs. Leeming sounded outraged. "You mean to tell me you think Mrs. Forst and that swaggie had anything in common? Taxes!" She flung herself back to her cooking.

Cherside echoed, "Taxes?"

"Too high. And what do they spend it on?" She rounded on him, wagging the egg slicer in front of his face, "Paying wages to the like of you! Waste!"

Mick gave a sudden rumble of laughter. He said lightly to the other man, "You watch out for her broom. I've seen her in action."

Rowena looked from one to the other in chilling thought. Did policemen always become like this when they were hunting? Mick had changed—he seemed to be one now with Cherside, with that calm affableness of Quince's. He was joking in the middle of fear; the hunter turning his back to the quarry, leading it to think he couldn't see what was under his nose.

She stood up. She said chillingly, "If you want me I'll be outside." To Mrs. Leeming she added, "No breakfast thanks." Her laughter mocked shrilly at their own jokes as she added, "I'm on a slimming diet!"

Quince was outside.

With Gregory, who was saying curtly, "If you don't want me any further I'll be getting on with the work." He gave Rowena a quick glance that seemed to hold warning, but he walked away without speaking to her.

Quince smiled at her. "Spare me a moment?" he suggested.

"I suppose so. Will we go inside?"

He rubbed his chin. "I don't think so. Marvellous the way you can hear up that chimney, isn't it?"

She knew her cheeks were burning. She jerked out, "How did you know?"

He gave a little chuckle. "I was in old Mrs. Forst's room last night, Rowena, and could hear what was being said down below."

So he had been in the house last night. While she had been sleeping. Perhaps he had even looked into her room and seen her lying there. And what had he been doing? she wondered.

Because she knew he wouldn't tell her; and because the silence was frightening, she asked, with seeming casualness, with an attempt at his own lightness, "And did you hear good of yourself, Inspector?"

"Ah, listeners never do and Miss Condrick's opinion of me isn't very high."

So it had been Linda speaking. To Gregory?

As though he read in her eyes what she was wondering he said, " Miss Wilma has quite a tongue when she's roused, hasn't she? "

So it had been Wilma and Linda. Quarrelling?

Quince was going on, " And then Dr. Paul doesn't think too highly of me either. Nearly had a fit that it could be suggested Mrs. Forst had died from anything but a heart attack following on a weakening illness. As he reminded me it takes two doctors to examine a dead person and issue certificates for cremation. And she was cremated, wasn't she, Rowena? "

" Yes. She always said that was what she wanted. She used to say she couldn't stand the idea of mouldering away in the darkness and . . ."

" Sensible really, but hard on the likes of us." His gaze was probing through her, dragging up all the fears in her, " because ashes don't hold any clues or answer any questions."

Ashes—ashes on a ridge that hid any traces of someone who had come and gone, leaving death behind. Ashes —scattered over the valley after a death that could never now be proved a natural one, or something else. One death a murder, they said. One death that could never be proved anything in particular.

And both since Linda had come to the valley.

" Who *is* Linda Condrick? "

That was Diana, asking the question in a hard, tight, controlled little voice that floated up the brick chimney to old Ella Forst's bedroom. Rowena didn't care if the police knew or guessed that she was up there. She had to know what was going on; had to know how the others fared with those endless questions about Ella's death; about that last week when the brooch had disappeared when Golden had camped by the billabong; when Ella had screamed at Linda, and died in the same night.

Quince was answering the question as though pleased he could give information in return for all he was asking.

"Miss Condrick is a fully trained nurse and a very good one. She was theatre sister at one of the largest Sydney hospitals until she resigned and came for a short while to Fobb's Creek as relieving sister there."

"Is that all you've found out?" Diana's disappointment was plain. "We know that already."

"What else did you expect?"

"I . . . oh, I don't know, but everything—all this trouble—has happened since *she* came. What do people say of her?" she asked eagerly. "People she's worked with and worked for and . . . what about private homes where she's nursed before. . . ."

Her voice gave away what she expected—that he would say, "People say she was greedy, grasping, going all out for what she could gain, in any way."

Her sigh, so deep the chimney caught it and flung it up to Rowena, followed on Quince's, "She never did any private nursing till she came here. Everyone speaks highly of her. A fine nurse. Just a bit too short with weakness and other people's fears."

"Yes. But a lot, lot more than just a bit. She's had to fight for things and she's only got contempt for people who can't fight the way she's done."

"Perhaps if you'd tossed around from one foster home to another and then been tossed out on your own when you were a teenager you might understand her," he suggested.

She denied feverishly, "I don't want to understand her! I want . . ." she was abruptly silent.

116

"You want to find out something bad about her—something that could cause her to be sent away from the valley? Did you take that brooch and hide it among her things?" he suddenly flung at her.

"I . . . oh no!" it came with utter conviction.

"Then perhaps you'd ask Miss Condrick if she would come in and see me?"

Diana must have stood up because her voice came from further away when she said bluntly, "I think you'd better send someone else for her. I don't know if I'm feeling shabby and acknowledging I could be wrong about her; or whether I want to claw her eyes out; but I don't want to face her."

The interview with Linda had been brief; a few short questions—"Are you certain, to your knowledge that Mrs. Forst died from a heart attack following on serious illness?" "Have you anything to add to your statement of last night?" "And you maintain you didn't know Golden?"— and three brief answers in Linda's cool voice, "Yes." "No." and again, "Yes," and then she was dismissed and it was Mrs. Leeming's turn.

The old lady said aggressively, "I'm not going to sit down. I don't want to and there's no time. I've work to do."

"So have I, so you sit down while I do it," Quince returned with a startling change to aggressiveness to match her own. Whether the change startled Mrs. Leeming so much as it did the listener in the room above Rowena didn't know, but at any rate Mrs. Leeming obviously accepted the chair and sat in silence, because Quince was back to affableness with, "What do you know about Mrs. Forst's death?"

"What do you think I am?" His aggressiveness hadn't quenched her in the least. "God? Or the Devil? They're the ones to ask about it. One or the other collected her and one or the other's got her now."

Quince gave a dry little chuckle that made his words so much colder in comparison, "But perhaps someone else knows? Someone who helped her on her way?"

"You're talking rubbish. It's only in books your own kith and kin kill you."

"But there was someone here not Mrs. Forst's kith and kin, wasn't there?"

"So it's nurse you're after." The words had a punctured sound, as though all the aggressiveness had abruptly gone.

Quince said, "You don't think she died anything but a natural death? I've seen her photo upstairs. Not the sort of old lady who'd take kindly to being crossed, was she? A cold old lady, I should have said? Given to outspokenness? And to demanding justice? Not someone to let things slide if she thought someone had stolen a piece of her jewellery for instance?"

Rowena, crouched and huddled over, could still look across the room; could still see the photograph of old Ella that stood on the dressing table. It was one Rowena herself had taken a couple of years before of Ella with Gregory. From it the old face peered out with level dark glance, the arrogantly pointed chin held high above the high, old-fashioned collar, the small mouth compressed in aloofness.

Mrs. Leeming was agreeing, "That's right."

"Did she say anything to you that she thought someone in house had taken it?"

"Didn't see her. Not that day."

"Did everyone in the family expect to share the valley under Mrs. Forst's will?"

"Ask them."

"But they were all surprised when they heard the will, weren't they?"

"Surprised!" The word came half jeeringly. "Surprised wasn't . . ." she stopped. Rowena could imagine the way the little wrinkled cherry of a mouth clamped shut on the words; could imagine the way it slackened in shock when Quince asked softly, "And did you expect something? For long service? Half a century of it? An annuity to pension you off in security?"

"What if I did?" but there was a quaver under the aggressiveness, a shock that she tried to deny with, "And Mr. Gregory wouldn't see me turned out."

"But would Miss Condrick feel the same way?"

"Ask her. I've never heard her speak against me."

CHAPTER XIII

"WHERE is Gregory?"

The question came reluctantly as though Linda grudged asking any help, even so slight a thing.

Rowena turned from her grooming of her own bay mare, and blew back her tumbled dark brown hair from where it was snaking in damp tendrils over her forehead.

"Somewhere. Didn't he tell you where he was going?"

"No," Linda admitted.

And that's something different, Rowena thought in sharp awareness, remembering how Gregory's concern since Linda's coming to the valley had made him always call to her where he was going, or call to one of the others, "Tell Linda . . ." so that Linda among them all was always aware of where he was. At first it had been so he could be summoned quickly if Ella wanted him; then it had been for Linda's own sake; for the sake of the new mistress.

Looking into the grey-irised eyes she knew that Linda too was remarking the fact that Gregory had gone for the first time without leaving any message for her.

Rowena said abruptly, "I gave Gregory a promise yesterday."

"What?"

"That I'd try to take care of you."

Linda stared at her, for once the blank expression giving place to sheer amazement. Then a hot tide of red came up under the olive skin. "Take care of me!" the voice lashed. "What are you supposed to do? Is Gregory too now using you as a spy? Rowena, follow her. Rowena, watch her. Rowena, report me everything she does or says. Rowena, watch to see she does no more harm! Is that it? "

Rowena was staring at her blank astonishment, in creeping dislike, in rising fear. Then the tide of colour was gone The tide of passion too. Linda's voice was cool as ever. Her face was expressionless as she looked beyond Rowena, and asked, " What do you want? "

Rowena whipped round, staring at the man who had come on them unheard. A little chunky man in overwashed cotton trousers and flannel shirt, he was smiling at them, showing yellowed teeth in a broad grin as he doffed his stained felt hat to reveal a mass of tight greying curls. The bright blue eyes surveyed them with good humour.

" Permission to camp out, missus. Just that."

Linda's mouth went suddenly stiff with memory.

Rowena eyed the man curiously, looking at the grey blanketed swag swinging from his shoulder. He wasn't a swaggie, but one of the men who were forever on the move from property to property, never staying long before restlessly drifting on. She had seen him before she realised and said, half accusingly, " You're from Crofts place the other side the town, aren't you? "

" Right, miss." He showed the yellowed teeth again in an appreciative grin. " John Dolley."

" Where are you off to now? "

" Nowhere in particular," he said vaguely though the bright blue eyes were gazing from one to the other of the women with sparkling interest, " Got any jobs you're . . ."

Linda said crisply, " No. Why do you want to camp here? "

He grinned at her. " Thought maybe tomorrow, next day, sometime, you'd have a truck goin' out somewhere. . . ."

" And you want a lift," Rowena broke in.

" Right." The grin threatened to become a permanent

yellow-toothed fixture on the seamed face. "All right, if I camp on the water?"

Linda said shortly, "If you want to."

He went away whistling, the old felt hat once more covering the tight grey curls. Linda asked, "Do you know him?"

"Vaguely. He was among the firefighters yesterday."

"Oh? Why should he leave his job at . . . Crofts, wasn't it, you said?"

"Yes. They often do. They just drift from place to place, but . . ."

"But what?" Linda was lighting a cigarette, her eyes half closed against the flame of her small gold lighter. The scene of a few minutes ago might never have happened at all.

"It's odd he should come right over here. I mean if he wants a lift why didn't he stay in town? Crofts is the other side of it. You'd have thought. . . ."

Linda said curtly, "Morbid fascination. He wants to see the spot where the body camped out." She turned on her heel and called back over her shoulder, "I can look after myself, Rowena. Even," the cool voice was cooler still, "if I have to shatter all of you."

Rowena was still grooming the bay mare when she became conscious that she was being watched. she looked up and they moved, crossing to her—two smiling-faced men moving with casual, even-lengthed strides, like casual visitors moving into her life, soon to be gone out of it.

When they stood close to her Quince reached out a hand and rubbed the mare's nose. He said, "The wind will be from the north tonight. Shipping's had a gale warning."

Instinctively her gaze went to the ridge, then to the high-riding brazen sun in the pale washed blue sky. "It might bring rain," she said hopefully, then added, "and we mightn't get much wind here— the coast might get it all."

"And you might get a gale force wind rushing through the valley and the house—much the sort of gale that went rushing through the place when that brooch went missing."

Here we go again, she though wearily, hating him.

He was saying, "Tell me again, Rowena, what happened when Mrs. Forst died. Who was with her?"

"No one. Not in the room. Linda was next door with the door open between the two rooms," she was speaking almost without thinking, because this was just repetition of what she had already told them. "She heard godmother call and ran in to her. The jaundice had made her very ill and very weak and she vomited a lot. That happened that night. And then she had a heart attack. Dr. Paul said it was partly exhaustion and partly shock from the upset."

"Over the brooch."

"Yes. Gregory rang the others and they all came over but there wasn't anything anyone could do except be around in case she woke and wanted to speak to us."

"Did she?"

"No."

"And then you all found you got nothing. Did *you* think at one time you'd get something?"

"Well, yes. But nothing much. I wasn't family. In any case I'm to get something—more, really, than I think she would ever have given me. That," she explained carefully, "is partly Linda's doing."

He said, "Perhaps Miss Condrick knew what the old lady wanted for you. She discussed it . . . Mrs. Forst I mean . . . with Gregory Forst, didn't she?"

"Yes, but she wouldn't have with Linda. Not then. . . ."

"But one day Mrs. Forst told her about the valley's history and about the family and she finished up by saying

123

everything was going to Gregory Forst on her death—to old Gregory Forst's only grandson."

She opened her mouth. Closed it. Stood waiting.

"Miss Condrick says the others knew—that was why she was certain they would do anything to get rid of her, even label her a thief, when they realised Gregory Forst wanted to marry her."

"But they didn't!" she cried. "Oh, if you'd seen their faces and anyway . . ." she frowned in puzzlement.

He said, "Of course, if they hadn't known, there wouldn't have been any reason for them to really worry about her—it wouldn't have mattered to them who Gregory Forst married—if the valley was divided into three."

She was gazing into blankness, seeing the shocked incredulous faces of the family listening to that brief will. Shocked. Incredulous. Disbelieving. None of them had known at all. It had shown in their faces, in their wild, shrill voices. Her lips parted, then pressed tight because that admission made of Linda a further liar; made of her whole story of the brooch and her actions a lie; but made her the holder of the knowledge that Gregory was to own the whole valley . . . *when* Mrs. Forst was dead.

She didn't say anything, then she knew that her tight-pressed lips and silence had given her away. Quince was nodding as though in satisfaction.

You could hear Billy's voice far above the sounds of the sheep, of Hudson's swinging hammer fixing the paddock gate that had worked loose on its hinges. Rowena, hearing it, felt cringing dislike and disgust for the whine in it, the whine of a beggar going cap in hand for charity. Just as might Golden have spoken coming to the kitchen door and asking if there was anything for him.

Billy was saying as Rowena approached the paddock

124

and the penned sheep and the three men, "We're entitled to know how we stand surely to God, Greg. It's not in you to leave a sheep in misery but, God damn it, you seem to be enjoying watchin' us squirm."

"Are you squirming?" Gregory's voice sounded almost disinterested. "Why? Because you know you're not worth much—not even the house you've been living in?"

Billy was almost spluttering in weak incoherent rage, "Not even worth . . . Hud, you heard him. Not even worth the house. After thirty years here. . . ."

"What have you done with them?" Gregory asked bluntly. "Sat down and dreamed. And talked. And got money out of Ella to throw away on investments that wouldn't have fooled a five-year-old. You got plenty out of her, Bill. Too much."

"And now you reckon we're not getting out of you—not getting anything of what you reckon's all yours?"

"It's mine. As you say. And like Linda—I don't like cadgers, Bill."

Rowena could see the big body starting to sag. He looked suddenly old, suddenly horribly pathetic in his ridiculous shorts showing the stick-thin legs; in the shivering of his pouted lower lip.

Hudson's hammer had never ceased in its work, till now, when Billy shuffled slowly back across the paddock, clambered stiffly over the far fence and went shambling towards the homestead. Then he said harshly, "You asked what he's done in those thirty years and damn-all's the answer good enough, but what about Di? She's worked on the place. So's Wilma."

"They were well paid. In allowances. In more. Paid every time they came to Ella with outstretched hands. And you, too."

Abruptly Hudson shouldered the hammer and went

striding away, vigorously, straight-backed, but once past the further fence, his big body started to sag as Billy's had done. Billy had seen him following. He stopped and stood waiting till Hudson came abreast of him. Rowena saw the two felt hats come close together, bend together, sway together in the windy words of whispered confidences. Then the two of them turned. They stood staring towards Gregory Forst. Heads close together. Bodies close together. Staring, their mouths grim and straight. Then Gregory looked up. As though the look touched a spring in them, two bodies sagged, two bodies turned, four feet went shuffling away.

Gregory shaded his eyes, looking towards Rowena. " Am I wanted? " he asked.

" No. I just came out to see if I could help." She pulled herself onto the top of the fence and asked, " Did you know the wind will be coming from the north tonight? "

" Yes. We're going up afterwards to see if we can make a break across part of the ridge, at least. The trouble is it's too long for anything really effective—if we save the middle it will get through at the ends and once away . . ."

She nodded. She had seen too many fires not to be able to picture it—a seeming lull and then the fire belching out and away in one great rush, leaping upwards into trees that threw sparks and burning branches far out into short summer-parched grass that instantly sprang into gleeful, orange-red life that went dancing away pursued by frantic men trying to thresh it out.

She said, " There's one extra hand on the place anyway. John Dolley—remember that man who was at Crofts for a little while? He's camping by the billabong till he gets a lift further out."

He was scowling. " Dolley! " his grimace expressed

nothing but disgust. "About as much help as Golden would be. Crofts was turning him loose, so he told me last week." He stood staring towards the billabong with squinted grey eyes as though trying, even at that distance, to see the man of whom they were speaking. "I'd like to know why he chose to come over here." Then he shrugged, "Curiosity, I expect. Use him for odd jobs if you want to, but don't let him into the house. And don't let him get hold of anything to drink—that was Crofts' main grievance about him."

"He could help on the ridge," she protested. "He was up here yesterday. I saw him once and . . ."

Gregory said, "Yes, I remember now. His name was on the check list." He was suddenly lost in thought.

"Gregory!" she shook at his shoulder when he went on staring into blankness.

He said, "I was just thinking that Dolley is the Golden type—he'd be just the sort to sneak off somewhere as soon as he'd done what he thought was enough and have a pleasant rest—especially if he had a bottle to keep him company. I wonder if he saw Golden or went near the gully?"

She said dryly, "If the police haven't asked him that they must be slipping. I bet they got out of him every time he blinked his eyes against the smoke and . . ."

"Nobody gets anything out of that type if they don't want it let out. I think I'll have a talk to him myself later on. Rowena—remember what you promised me?"

"Yes. I told Linda I promised. I . . . don't think she was pleased. She said she can look after herself. And after all what can I do—even if I keep silent about anything he seems to know. That Quince. And . . . oh, Greg, it's as they all say—who *is* Linda Condrick? What does anyone know about her? Even you? Except that she came here and, as she admits herself, she saw you and the homestead and all the valley and wanted them all."

Marcia had come downstairs again, with shrill complaints that her knee was still paining her, but once settled in the long chair in the living-room she seemed to forget it in the reading of yet another paper-backed love novel, her brittle-gold hair fanned out against the cushion behind her head.

It wasn't till Rowena passed her for the third time in moving back and forth between kitchen and living-room that she realised Marcia wasn't reading at all. The book in her hands remained open at page eleven and from its shield her eyes were darting little measuring, angry, watchful glances at Linda who was working on the valley correspondence, a job she had taken over with cool efficiency the previous week when she had found Gregory struggling in a maze of official forms.

Abruptly Marcia snapped out, thrusting her head suddenly forward over the book like a suspicious turtle thrusting out of its shell, "Who was that man who came and spoke to you and Rowena, Linda?"

Linda looked up. "Man?" she said vaguely. "Oh, some chap wanting to camp until he got a lift further on. I forget his name. Ask Rowena if you're interested."

Rowena paused on her way to the kitchen.

"John Dolley. You don't know him, Marcia. He was at Crofts for a while."

Marcia pulled a face at her. "Send him away!" she said with surprising viciousness. "I hate those men who move on all the time. They're like gypsies. Swaggies. Not much difference," her darting gaze had returned to Linda.

Rowena objected, "He's doing no harm. Anyway he can move on tomorrow probably and he might be handy if the

128

fire breaks out again tonight. He helped yesterday, though Gregory doesn't seem to think he would have done much. He thinks like you, Marcia, that there's hardly a scrap of difference between Dolley's type and Golden and that perhaps Dolley went off to sleep too. Maybe near the gully. Anyway he's going to ask him."

She was conscious of a stillness—all through the house —all through the women who had turned to watch her— Linda and Marcia in the living-room and Mrs. Leeming and Wilma from the kitchen. Even Diana from the verandah, where her pale face showed for a minute on her way round to the kitchen doorway.

CHAPTER XIV

WILMA and Mick Gambell had had a flaming quarrel that had started when he came back just before dinner to report everything was so far quiet on the ridge, but men would be watching all night. Wilma had greeted him with a sudden lifting of the sullen darkness that had been on her face all day, inviting, "Come and sit down, Mick. Dinner will be on in ten minutes and afterwards . . ."

He had said quietly, "I'm sorry. I can't stop."

"Why not?" she had flashed back, banging plates down onto the dining-room table.

He had said something about work and Rowena had listened then in appalled silence to the row that had stormed up, with Wilma shrieking at him, "So it offends you to sit down with the guilty? You don't like eating salt in Leumeah any more?"

Mick had told her not to be stupid and Wilma had burst into tears. Diana had made things worse by rushing to her daughter's defence, crying out to Mick that if he thought the family were guilty he could go and not come back.

Mick had finished it with a furious, "I'm beginning to think I could believe anything of any of you," and flung out.

Rowena ran after him. "Mick, oh please. . . ."

He stopped. He looked embarrassed and worried.

"That sounded like the nursery, didn't it? It's a wonder one of us didn't stick out our tongue and yell, 'Yah— stinker!' at the other. But . . . oh hell, Rowena, what's got into them all?" Then he shrugged, "Oh I know, well enough. Linda Condrick. Do you know what Wilma said to me this morning? That Linda Condrick is like a deadly snake. She's crept into the place and she's curled up waiting to strike unless they strike first and get rid of her. They're all afraid and nobody's normal when they're afraid."

She stood there, watching the car's tail-light become a spark in the distance across the valley. Not normal, she thought. And that was right. But Linda wasn't normal either. All that coldness. All that calmness. That wasn't normal for anything except something that had no real emotions—something, she thought suddenly, like a snake. Wilma was right. And when snakes struck, they sometimes killed.

Rowena turned sharply back towards the house, then stopped. In the dusk she saw Dolley near the stables.

She called sharply, "What are you doing there?"

In the dusk his face was shadowed as he came across to her. He was wearing the greasy felt hat though the sun had gone. It added to the shadow on his face, but she could clearly see the yellow-toothed grin.

"Spare a bit of sugar, miss?" he said with the easy asking of a bushman requesting the open-handed bush hospitality. There was nothing of the cringing whine below the note of bluster that many of the swaggies used in his request, but she was remembering what Gregory had said about him as she hesitated.

The smile seemed to grow broader and broader across the seamed shadowed face as he waited. Then Linda's voice called to them both. She was near the stables. Rowena realised then that Linda hadn't heard or seen that row between Wilma and Mick. She had disappeared somewhere before that.

Now she said, "Who is it?"

"Dolley, missus." He turned to her, "Just came up to say I was outa sugar. I was just askin' for sugar this time."

Linda said, "Go to the kitchen. I'll give it you there." She came forward and stepped up to the verandah. Dolley stood still till she began to move round to the kitchen, then he walked below her on the ground, looking up at her, smiling.

Everyone had gone to bed early, eagerly. Not only, Rowena knew, to shut out the constant circling of eyes; the constant silent questioning and doubts of each other; but because they snatched greedily at the chance of sleep while it was possible, before the wind might strengthen from the north and shake the three homesteads in the valley, and stir the top layer of ash on the ridge and reach down to the hot jewels of sparks below, stirring them, spreading them, tossing them upwards and downwards in swirling points of light.

The McGuires rattled away to the foot of the ridge in their old battered car, and Hudson left after seeing Marcia upstairs at the main homestead. Rowena went inside when the rear lights on his car were bobbing points of light in the distance and sent Mrs. Leeming upstairs, before going up herself.

She looked in on Marcia, who gazed at her over the rim of the paper-backed love novel and said shortly, "No, I don't want anything. Except see Linda Condrick out of here."

She didn't look in on Linda, and Gregory hadn't come in, she knew. She stood by her window, listening for his footsteps on the stairs, but they didn't come. Instead a flicker of torchlight showed dancing away from the homestead, and past the stables; went dancing and flickering and jerking in the direction of the billabong.

Rowena hesitated, then abruptly she went running out and downstairs. Out of the house, following the light ahead on its journey until it was lost in the radiance of another light and she stood near the two gum trees a little distance from the water and its weeping willows, looking into the radiance of a camp-fire shining on a seamed, smiling face.

Dolley was singing to himself in a cracked, slurring voice that made the words unintelligible to Rowena. He didn't stop singing when his visitor made his appearance, switching off his torch as he said, "Evening, Dolley."

"Evenin', Mr. Forst." Dolley grinned upwards, his singing quietened. He reached forward to throw another stick on the fire and the flames went leaping upwards, curling round the blackened billy that hung above it with the steam rising out of the top of it.

"Stamp that fire out before you go to sleep," Gregory said curtly, squatting down on his heels on the other side of it. "The wind's coming up and I don't want any fire near the homestead or in the valley tonight."

"Comin' from the north." Dolley lifted his head, seemed to be sniffing the air. "No rain in't though."

"More's the pity. The whole ridge is still smouldering. You helped out yesterday, didn't you?" the question was suddenly shot out.

"Yeah. Bumped into you once or twice. Warm, wasn't it?" He gave a sudden rumbling chuckle of laughter.

"Too warm for comfort. I expect you found it so and that's why I didn't see you after the first couple of hours. I expect you made off somewhere back of it."

The grin remained. "Who's sayin' I might've?"

"I am. And any other man who knows you. Crofts was turning you off, wasn't he? For laziness. Sneaking off with a bottle when you should have been working. Lazy men

133

don't like fires, Dolley. Or fighting them, when it's no loss to them if the sheep burn."

The grin remained, as though rigidity had set in, and there was no way of removing it; as though it had been put there across the seamed features and completely forgotten.

Dolley didn't speak. Just smiled and looked at the rising steam and the leaping flames.

Gregory went on in that same conversational tone, "Golden found the gully a pleasant place to rest in. The smoke wasn't there till well on in the afternoon. It was the sort of place you'd make for yourself if you knew of it, and you've often been round this way, haven't you? You'd be hidden from anyone passing by, too. I think you spent a fair portion of the day there, lying comfortably in the grass. Just like Golden."

The flames were dying a little and as though they were a screen, a protection, between him and retribution, Dolley reached forward and threw more sticks on the fire—too many, so that the flames went leaping up, hiding the blackened billy altogether, the light leaping and playing shadow games over the seamed, smiling face.

Gregory said, "It's odd you should come here—pass through town and head into the valley. Your type usually avoids anywhere there's police and we've too many of them about here for comfort. So why come? Unless you thought there was something for you here—something you knew that could be paid for in cash."

Rowena drew in a deep breath, shifting a little, trying to see Gregory's face. But there was only the dark outline of his squatting figure the other side of the leaping flames.

He was saying, "There's no cash in it for you, Dolley—for whatever you're going to hint you know. But there's going to be trouble for you if you don't choose to speak out."

Dolley spoke for the first time, "Meanin'? "

"The sheep are in the home paddocks. A man has fancied fresh meat before this and taken it. You have in the past. How long did you get last time? Not as long as for a third or fourth offence anyway. Ask yourself if what you think you know is worth as much as a prison sentence. If the answer's 'yes' I'll supply the evidence of a butchered sheep and ring Mick Gambell."

There was silence.

"Keep asking yourself," Gregory said softly.

Dolley said, "I was asleep. That's gospel. Away down past Golden. I wasn't having any of'm. Then I woke up. I saw two of them come into the gully. . . ."

His face, with the moving mouth, was there in the camp-fire light and then not there, jerked backwards, as the shot came crashing from the darkness, then bending, bowing forward in a gentle grace, the light flaring over the tight grey curls for an instant before he fell completely. Some part of his falling body—perhaps on outstretched defending hand—must have touched the fire, because a cloud of sparks danced upwards in swirling abandon towards the trees bending above the fire, Rowena saw in that moment as the shot sent her flat to the trunk of the tree behind her and left Dolley bowing his salute to death.

She saw the dark squatting figure come up, become a huge shadow jerking and bending in the camp-fire light, then she fled—on silent feet across the summer-dried grass, towards the homestead.

She went through the open windows of the living-room and across the shadowed silence of the room and silently, in pulse-beating horror and panic, to the shadows of her room. She was shaking all over. There could never, never be any more hope of claiming a death an accident, or a death as natural. A man had died before her eyes in dancing camp-fire light because he had seen too much. And his death was murder.

She was there, still shaking, still pressing her hands over her eyes, trying to blot out the smiling face, the graceful bow to conquering death; trying not to think when steps came softly up the stairs. Softly, but not too softly for sharpened nerves of fear to catch.

Rowena stood listening against her door. There was a soft pitter-patter, a slither, a whisper of movement. Gently she eased open her door. The landing was dark but her eyes were used to darkness now. And then somewhere below there were running steps, urgent steps, crashing through the house with no concealment.

The sound of them jerked Rowena's gaze towards the stairs for one instant. When she looked back, her gaze searching the darkened landing, there was nothing. Only the darkness and a row of closed doors.

CHAPTER XV

THEY were all there, a huddled group drawn not together by tragedy, but apart. Each of them stood or sat alone, separated by suspicious space on either side as they watched, eyes moving from side to side to gaze corner-wise but never directly, at those who stood or sat on either side beyond that protecting space in which each had islanded himself. Gregory had told them nothing when he had rung the two other houses. He had said only, "You're needed. Come at once," and to Billy, in the house at the foot of the ridge, he had added, "all three of you."

Then he had come upstairs and roused them—the four women who shared his home that night. He still said nothing, only, "Come down. You're needed."

Rowena had wanted to cry, "I know!" but appalled silence held her. The silence of knowledge. That one of the other three had been out in the darkness; had come silently through the silent house and gone into her room; and come downstairs, apparently newly roused from sleep, eyes wondering, mouth questioning.

When they were all assembled Gregory had told them. Of going to the billabong; of speaking to Dolley; of seeing him die. And slowly. in little inching movements, body had sidled from body; husband from wife; daughter from parents; cousins from cousins; friend from friends; and all of them sidling into a further islanding—from the stranger in the house.

Linda knew it.

It was betrayed in her going towards the mantelpiece; in

her stance; head back defiantly; her watchful silence. She was waiting for open attack instead of those sidling glances and moving mouths that went from tongue moistening thought to pouting doubt, to indrawn suspicion and worse, without saying a word.

It was Marcia, a Japenese silk kimono of lotus-flowered embroidery, over green nylon nightgown, who tossed the first stone with a hissing, "Say where you were, Linda."

It boomeranged back in soft enquiry, "Where were *you*, Marcia?"

The blue eyes jerked wide in astonishment and fury.

"Me? Look at me!" She pulled up the froth of nylon skirt and the embroidered silk and thrust out the bandaged knee, "Look at that and then ask again!"

Linda said, "You've said a lot about that knee, but you haven't asked for a doctor. And desperation's a miraculous remedy."

Hudson's face had reddened. He started forward and Gregory stepped into his path.

He said, "The Police are on their way. From Fobb's Creek. They said to bring everyone here to the main homestead and keep you here. I've done it. You're not leaving and you'd better not speak, until they get here."

The boss had cracked the whip of authority, Rowena thought disgustedly, and now the dependent sheep were bleating obedience that started with Billy's, "Only sensible," and Diana's nodding sidelong glance at Linda, "There'll be plenty of time," and Wilma's sullen, "We'll be sick enough of talking soon," went on to Hudson's curt, "If others are quiet I'll stay quiet," and Marcia's reminding, "And the police will ask what I want to know anyway," to finish in Mrs. Lemming's shaky, "You'll all dig your graves with your tongues if you don't watch."

They sat. Simply sat. And all of them watched Linda.

138

The minutes went dragging on, then Mick came through the doors from the verandah and behind like Siamese twins, close together, step by step together, came Quince and Cherside, as affable, as considerate as ever, with Quince's opening, "Now don't stand about. Make yourselves comfortable as you can, because I'm afraid I may have to keep you up for quite a while."

"Otherwise, of course," Wilma snapped, "we'd all go back to bed and go peacefully to sleep! After all we ought to be used to sudden death by this time."

Quince paid no attention to her. Neither did Cherside, but Mick crossed to her, to stand by her chair. She ignored him sullenly. Then abruptly her hand went out, catching at his, and his closed tightly over the slim fingers.

Cherside had brought two chairs and set them side by side near the verandah door. Only two, because the next minute Quince was asking Mick to go down to the billabong again and stay there.

Again . . . which meant they had already looked over the scene on their way to the homestead. But there was nothing out there in the dark except a dying camp-fire and a dead man and the sheep that even in darkness weren't still. There was nothing to hurt the dead when Quince was sure the person he would finally take away with him was here in the room. So why send Mick back into the darkness, unless it was because Quince had seen the younger man's twisted angry face as he looked round the circle of people he had once called friends, seeing the way their faces turned to his hopefully, expectant of comfort and help.

When he had gone Quince and Cherside took the chairs by the door and Quince asked, "Now where was everyone when Dolley died? Gambell got your call, Mr. Forst, at five minutes to ten. Where were you all?"

Marcia laughed. Her gaze flicked towards Linda.

Linda took up the challenge with a quiet, "I was in bed. I went up at a quarter past nine. We all turned in early because of the fire."

There was a little ripple through the room—a ripple of shocked surprise and movement as bodies turned in an effort to see the ridge—a ripple of astonishment that they, so deeply linked with elemental things, should have, even for a few minutes, forgotten the ridge.

Remembrance jerked from Hudson, "The wind was strengthening when I came over."

They all sat silently and for the first time Rowena saw Quince disconcerted and faintly shocked. She looked at him, her teeth in her lower lip. He looked back steadily, then his gaze went on to Linda. His eyes half closed as though the silence had lulled him into resting, but when she looked back at him they were open again, on herself, a faint expression of something like amusement in them.

She looked quickly away, at the others, so islanded in suspicion. Fire's coming would have welded them together; Linda's coming had thrust them apart. They would go on moving apart now until Quince put out his hand and said, "Come with me."

She wished, in desperate intensity, that, as Quince had once wished, the swagman's ghost could be heard speaking by the billabong—that he could be heard telling how Linda had come from the smoke to place the enamelled pannikin in his hand.

Because that was how it had been. Hadn't it? Her eyes asked and got no answer.

The question repeated itself over and over in thought as she listened to the McGuires speaking of going home and to bed; to Hudson telling how he had entered his silent home and gulped down a long draught of icy milk while staring up at the ridge before turning out the lights and going to bed, too. She listened to Mrs. Leeming's impatient asking, "You think, do you, that at my age I go creeping out killing people?" and to Marcia asking, "And what about my knee? Can you see me? Of course I was in bed."

But one of them, Linda or Marcia or even Mrs. Leeming, was lying. And Rowena lied herself. She couldn't speak out about what she had seen and later heard. She was frightened too. She said, "I was in bed."

She listened to Gregory telling of the conversation he had with Dolley and was amazed that he could remember so clearly. She found herself wondering if before he had gone to the billabong he had thought out everything he would say and burned the words on memory. She tried not to listen when he spoke of Dolley's death, but she heard Quince say:

"So Dolley saw two people come down to the gully. Two people. . . ."

Wilma moved forward. Her gaze was on Linda. "Golden and one other person. And the other one Dolley intended to get money out of. He came up here tonight. Just before dinner that was; Rowena was outside and he asked her for sugar and then Linda spoke. I could hear her. I heard her ask what he wanted and he said, 'Just some sugar . . . this time. This time'," she repeated softly. "But would he have asked for sugar next time, Linda? He was speaking to *you* then, Linda—not Rowena. He said . . ."

Gregory said, "Linda . . ." as though in appeal, but his voice was drowned in the babble of outraged voices snapping and snarling at the tall girl by the mantelpiece.

Out of the centre of it came Billy's triumphantly voiced memory, "Remember how she bowled over that pig the day we took'r out? Right smack a'tween the eyes."

He stood looking at her, licking his lips a little, his eyes shining.

Rowena saw the flaming fear that came into the wide eyes, as though Linda was realising for the first time that they were many to her one; that however she might strike out and push one back the others would be there to give the first time to recover while they struck in turn themselves.

Rowena stood up. She said shakily, "That was a fluke. This would have needed . . ."

"This would have needed a Linda," Marcia triumphed. "You shouldn't have said that, Rowena. About a fluke. I was furious that day when she brought down that pig and I'd muffed all my shots. I said to her, 'Fluke!' and she said, 'Believe it or not, that wasn't. I learned to shoot when I was twelve. One of my foster homes was a farm and I learnt it the best way. If I didn't bring home something for the pot each time I went out, I went supperless to bed. My foster father said it was the way he learned and the best way. It was too. Because I'm a good shot now—really good,' and her eyes damned me to prove she wasn't. She had to shoot to eat. I guess she could shoot even better . . . to stay alive and free."

"Yes," Rowena agreed nervously. The police had sent the others away—into the dining-room—and she was alone with Quince and Cherside in the living-room as she admitted "I knew Gregory was going to speak to Dolley and I told the others, and I guess I did wrong, but I didn't honestly think Dolley would know anything. It was . . . I just wanted to . . . to needle them. To watch their faces."

"And try and play detective," Quince said. "All right, where did it get you?"

"Nowhere," she answered wretchedly, "they all looked up and stared but no one said anything."

142

"Who was here when you said it?"

"All of us—the women I mean. Mrs. Leeming and . . . Wilma, I think—yes, that's right . . . were in the kitchen and Linda and Marcia in the living-room and I remember Diana was looking in through the window—at the clock I think."

"Is Miss McGuire telling the truth, to your memory, about Dolley's visit to the house just before dinner?"

"Yes, but he didn't stress the words 'this time' the way Wilma did. He just rattled them off as though he was saying, 'Remember I came up before and asked permission to hang around and this time I'd be obliged for a bit of sugar',"

"He wasn't unpleasant?"

"Oh heavens no. He was smiling and . . . in fact I was thinking when he went away that Gregory had said he wasn't much above the swaggie type, but he had a bushman's ease in asking hospitality—I guess you wouldn't know —but it's a sort of assurance—not expecting to get refused sort of manner."

He said, "Ease in asking could be because you know that if you're refused you've got something up your sleeve to turn refusal into agreement—something that could get you a whole lot more than a bit of sugar."

She said coldly, "I never said that. I said . . ."

"Why didn't you go with Mr. Forst to see Dolley?" he broke in.

She said sulkily, "Why should I have? I told you I hadn't thought he knew anything and actually I'd forgotten about him and I was waiting for Gregory to come up and go to bed." She reddened. "I wanted to know he was here— I felt . . . oh, safer . . . knowing he was here." She hurried on, "Everyone was talking at dinner about the possibility of the wind blowing the fire up again and I forgot about Dolley."

She bit the last word off short. Just in time to stop herself adding, "Until I saw Gregory go down that way and I went down after him . . ." But the unspoken words remained there in her thoughts, cluttering them, clouding them, so that his next question nearly caught her off guard.

"Why was Miss Condrick out of the house?"

"How . . she wasn't. She said so. She never said she was outside."

"Neither does my old Tom cat, but by all the kittens wearing his face I've seen in our street he goes just the same. Sure she wasn't out?"

"How should I know? I was . . ."

"You were waiting for Mr. Forst to come up to bed. And he didn't come."

She stared at him, then said slowly, "I went to bed. When I didn't hear anything I thought perhaps he'd come up before. . . ."

"Oh no, he said pleasantly, "that won't wash, to put it vulgarly. You were waiting for Mr. Forst to come up so you could feel safe and go peacefully to sleep. You've told us so. Do you mean to tell us now that five minutes later you suddenly felt all suddenly safe and peaceful even when you didn't know if he'd gone right out or where he was?"

He kept on and on at her and now he wasn't pleasant at all. And Cherside, the witness, she remembered, sat there and wrote it all down—all Quince's questions and her wrigglings and evasions till she confessed she had seen Gregory go and followed him.

Then he returned to pleasantness. He said, "It's always better to tell the truth in the first place. Now—someone else was outside too, weren't they?"

"How did you know that?" she whispered.

"Who was it?" was the only answer she got.

She shook her head, "You can ask all night and I can't

answer you because I don't know. But footsteps came up the stairs after me and I looked out, and then I heard Gregory running downstairs. I looked away from the landing for hardly any time at all and when I looked back there wasn't anyone there at all."

Then she saw what he was holding between his fingers. She stared, fascinated. He said, "Down by the billabong. Still sure you didn't see anyone? Positive? Certain? Definite? Like to think again? Positive about that? Certain? Definite? And you don't know where the person went? What room? Positive? Definite? Certain about that?"

He went on and on, gently repeating, gently pounding on already raw nerves. In the end he nodded and said, "All right, Rowena, you may go," and tossed the gold lighter onto the table in front of him.

Linda's lighter.

He had them all in the living-room again. The lighter was still on the table. Linda had lost it. So she said. She couldn't remember where or when. But Billy said triumphantly, "You had it in your hand when Di and I left. You were lighting a cigarette and watching Greg say goodbye to us."

And suddenly the mask cracked. Linda slumped down into a chair. She said, "All right. It's no good. I'll tell you. I was there. I heard everything he said. Everything Gregory said. And I saw him die. I was lighting a cigarette when the shot came—from somewhere at the back of me I think. It frightened me so much I dropped the lighter. I tried and tried to find it," her doubled fists pounded on her knees in frantic desperation, "and I couldn't and I knew Gregory would rouse the house in a minute. I had to leave it and run."

" What were you doing down there? " Quince demanded.

"Listening. I've told you. From the moment Rowena wondered aloud this afternoon why Dolley had by-passed the town and come over here looking for a lift I wondered . . . if he knew something. About . . . someone here. I wanted to talk to him myself. But I had to wait till the others had gone and the house was quiet. I saw Greg leave. And I followed."

She straightened a little. " I've nothing else to say," she finished almost arrogantly.

Quince nodded. He said quite pleasantly, " I must ask you to pack your things and return to Fobb's Creek with me."

Rowena watched in appalled fascination. Everyone moved. Bodies straightened, mouths smiled, eyes gleamed and hands reached out, one to another in congratulation, in comfort, in sharedness.

Only Linda remained, islanded in isolation. Then she wasn't alone either. Because Gregory stepped to her side. He said, " No! Linda. . . ."

She reached up and touched his hand. They looked at one another and words seemed to flow silently from one to another. Then she said too, " No. I'm going to speak out. I didn't want to. I hoped . . ."

Quince began to warn her. The words fell heavily into silence. She brushed aside the warning.

" It's gone too far. I must have been mad. . . ." Now her calmness seemed completely gone. She looked distracted as she gazed at them. Into the silence she said, " One of you tried to kill me."

Rowena looked at her in wonderment; at the others; at the police. She saw distraction, astonishment, no expressions at all.

Linda was going on, " I know nothing about Golden. Absolutely nothing and that's the truth. That day when

146

he came here everything was just as I said it was. Up to the time I was due to come down again. And before that—about the brooch—everything I said about that was the truth, too. One of you hates me. Or it might be two of you, or all of you!"

She looked round at them in blazing anger, her grey eyes wide and dark. She moistened her lips with the tip of her tongue and seemed to be collecting her thoughts, then in a quieter voice she said, "I went up to the ridge and I was helping hand food to the men and to give what small amount of first-aid was needed. I was moving around all the time, speaking sometimes to some of the men, seeing you . . ." her eyes flicked round at the family, "sometime, too. Time passed so quickly I was honestly astonished when I realised it was after three o'clock in the afternoon. Gregory told me. He told me I was looking tired—that I must *be* tired and that I was to go down and rest. When I protested he told me the fire was getting worse and that unless the wind came from the south and helped it might be completely out of hand that night and that I, as a nurse, might be called on to deal with serious injuries. He was still speaking to me and urging me to go when Rowena came along. Gregory spoke to her and asked her to see that I went down and rested for a while.

"I was furious! He looked exhausted himself and I felt I was capable of doing what I could for quite a while, if he was capable of doing a harder job without a break. And it also galled me to have a child Rowena's age put over me to act as a sort of sheep dog!"

She looked briefly at Rowena. The look held the faintest touch of apology for a moment, or so it seemed to Rowena, then Linda's chin lifted arrogantly again as she went on steadily, "I simply walked away from her and lost her. Which was a pity. Because if ever anyone had needed a guardian sheep dog it was I right then. I disappeared into the smoke to get rid of her, though she called to me, and I went working along the line of men again till I seemed to be on my own. Then suddenly smoke came billowing out at me and I saw the fire—it was quite a distance from me but it was a terrible thing. The smoke had belched out from it towards me. I didn't have anything over my face then and in seconds my eyes were watering terribly and I was coughing and . . . almost ill . . . and then suddenly someone pushed a pannikin of tea into my hand and a voice said huskily, 'Drink up'." Her gaze went to Hudson as though she was remembering how he had suggested the words a person might use to another coughing in the smoke.

"I turned round to thank whoever it was, but my eyes were watering so badly all I saw was a vague figure disappearing into the smoke. There was no need to go after them. I knew vaguely where I was. I thought suddenly I was near that gully and I thought of lying down and drinking that hot tea—it was a lovely thought. If it hadn't been for that—the thought of resting in peace and drinking leisurely, I would probably have gulped at the tea there and then. As it was I held the pannikin and went out through the smoke and right ahead of me was the gully— the perfect place for some tired person to rest for a while.

"I was nearly there when Golden rose up out of it. He scared me for a minute—he was an awful looking old brute. And he had his eyes on the pannikin. He said in a blustering fashion, 'How about a drink?' Something like that anyway and his gaze was shifting around to make sure none of the men were with me. I frankly admit he scared me. And I was furious too. It was obvious he hadn't done one thing to help—that he had been lying there in comfort all day. I thought of Gregory, and the other men—for a

148

minute . . . I nearly threw the tea in his face." Abruptly her hands went up to press over her eyes as though the memory of that day's events was before her eyes and she didn't want to see it—couldn't bear to. Then her hands dropped back to her lap again. She said, " All my feeling of peace—in the thought of resting in the gully—was gone And I didn't want the tea either. I pushed it at him and he grinned and mumbled something and grabbed it and gulped. He knew, of course, something was wrong, but it was too late. Probably if my lungs hadn't been full of smoke I would have smelt something odd about the tea while I was carrying it, but maybe I wouldn't. He kept hold of the pannikin and . . . staggered back . . . away from me . . . trying to say something.

" I thought for a minute it was some sort of fit. When I put out my hand to him he looked at me . . . he was terrified. He went staggering back again and collapsed. I couldn't do a thing to help him. He was gone before I'd turned him over—he'd rolled onto his face—and looked at him. The pannikin was under him and I smelt it and knew . . . someone had tried to kill me."

Her gaze, searching, angry, went round the circle of watching faces again.

" There wasn't anything to be done for him. He was dead, and I was terrified. I've always prided myself on my self-control. I didn't have any then. All I could think of was getting off that ridge before whoever it was tried again some way.

" I jumped back to the lip of the gully and I fled. Rowena was quite right about that. I must have looked half crazy. And I completely forgot she was supposed to be going down with me. All I could think of was getting away. I jumped into the station wagon and tore down the track and back at the homestead I fled up to my room and threw things into my case—the jewellery Gregory had given me—my clothes—the first things my hands picked up. I took the case down and threw it into the car—Ella's car, that Gregory had given me.

"And then I suddenly realised that I couldn't just go like that and leave Gregory without a word. Leave him in possible danger himself. I'd have to wait till he came down and then talk to him—get him to take me away—marry me immediately. I had some vague plan of making the others all leave the valley before we came back. Perhaps I was so crazy I couldn't think straight, but . . . I hardly spared a thought for that poor creature in the gully.

"The waiting gave me a chance to get back some of my self-control, but of course I was acting oddly. The others were quite right about that. I couldn't keep still, and I couldn't stop looking at them, wondering, 'Was it you?' and I couldn't stop talking.

"The more I quietened, the more I planned. I thought that if I told the truth, the police would come—it was going to be sheer hell. I thought, I'll tell Gregory alone—we'll try and keep it in the family itself—we can possibly pass things off as an accident. I thought perhaps the fire would go over the gully—I suppose that was what was planned for me—I'd die and be put in the path of the fire and everyone would think, 'She was a city girl—the new chum' and weep crocodile tears over me."

Her gaze went round them again, as though asking this time, "Did *you* think that?"

"When the fire was over it seemed impossible to get Gregory alone. The men all came down—the house was crowded—there was almost a party air about the place. Then Mrs. Leeming spoke about the tramp. I still couldn't get Gregory alone. And finally I decided not to say anything. I was sure everyone would think his death an accident. I wasn't even going to tell Gregory and give him that horrible knowledge of what one of his family had done. I was going to sit it out myself. Get him to marry me as quickly as possible. Get him to send them all away. Perhaps . . . oh, there's no perhaps about it! I *was* afraid, too, that perhaps he wouldn't believe me. They'd been on on his back so much, hinting things about me, wanting me to go. If I said one of them had tried to kill me, would he really believe me? "

She suddenly turned, looking up at him. He didn't say anything and she turned sharply away.

She said, looking steadily at Quince, " Rowena told me she'd seen me run down the gully and drive away like someone who'd gone off their head. I tried to get out of her where everyone had been, but she didn't know, of course. She had been trying to find me and obey Gregory. She'd come up with Mrs. Leeming and Marcia though. And Diana had come up before them. She didn't know where Billy or Hudson were. The only one who wasn't on the ridge was Wilma McGuire. She'd been left at the homestead to answer any phone calls; speak to callers.

" I couldn't confide in Wilma though. She hates me as all of them do. She wouldn't have believed in me even if I was willing to speak out and let her live with the knowledge that someone—her parents perhaps—had tried to kill me.

" And then you came," she nodded to Quince. " And we knew it wasn't going to be called an accident. I'd let things go for so long that I wasn't game to speak out by that time. You'd be no more likely to believe me than they would, and I could just see them pouncing on the fact I'd handed that poor wretch the tea, and claiming I'd done it deliberately.

"And then things got worse. The affair of the brooch was turned against me. You tried to connect me with that and with Golden and even with Mrs. Forst's death. And now that other man is dead. . . ."

Her slim hands moved. Gracefully. Dismissingly. And then lay at rest in her lap again. She was waiting for them to speak, but the whole room was silent.

Then as one they moved. The family. Hudson said, "I've never heard such rot! You're on the run now, aren't you, Linda Condrick? Shifting and turning and trying to remove suspicion from your back."

Diana said, "I ought to be furious. For everything you've said. Trying to shift blame to us. Saying what you have. But I'm not. I agree with Hudson and do you know . . ." she leaned forward, her eyes intent, "suddenly I'm sorry for you, Linda Condrick. I pity you, Linda Condrick. Even after all you've done to us—to my aunt—to those two poor devils. Whatever you've got in your past that Golden knew about it must have rested on you . . . you like . . ." She shook her head, pressing back in her seat again.

Wilma began harshly, "I'm not sorry for her. You and your pretty speeches, Linda Condrick!" Her voice mimicked, "'. . . even if I were willing to let her live with the knowledge that her parents had tried to kill me . . .' how kind of you, Linda Condrick!"

Billy said, "I'll tell you what happened, Linda Condrick. Golden had somethin' on you and he came here and saw you sitting pretty and he wanted a share and you tried to pay him off with that brooch and old Ella found you out and you had to quieten'er too. Didn't you, Linda Condrick? And then Golden came back for money in place of the brooch, didn't he, and you didn't have money —not yet you didn't—and you killed him and got it back. And now you've killed John Dolley into the bargain and . . ."

Mrs. Leeming's voice came high and quavering across his shrill bitterness, "Are you going to take her away with you? Are you?"

Marcia snapped, "No one on earth's going to believe that rigmarole, Linda Condrick. I think, like Di, I'm even a bit sorry for you. What did Golden have on you?"

Linda's head went up. She said, "I've told the truth. One of you tried to kill me."

Marcia laughed. Her voice mocked, "Look at us, Linda Condrick. Are we frightened of what you've said?"

Linda's gaze moved. So did Rowena's. And she saw that Marcia was right. None of them were frightened. They were gazing back at Linda with glances that held spite and malice, pleasure and greed, a little pity, sick shrinking at the sight of her. But there was no fear in those faces.

Then she realised that something was moving close to her. She half turned. And looked at Mrs. Leeming. And stared blankly. The little rigid body was shaking with an ague that rocked the chair in which she sat, gaze fixed on Linda. Rowena moved a little, leaning forward, so that her own body hid the old trembling one, while thought went riot; questioned and answered and discarded the answers and sought for others. She didn't look round again. Only leaned forward like that, her body a screen, while the little rigid figure so screened went on trembling.

Quince was saying, "If you're to be believed, Miss Condrick, the whole investigation will have to start again."

There was immediate uproar. They were all yelling at him. He just stared at them till finally they quietened. Then he said, "For the time being, Miss Condrick, you will remain here in this house. I want everyone to stay here. I will arrange with Gambell to have your things packed and brought to you here. None of you are to leave this home-stead. I am awaiting certain information from Sydney. I may have it by the morning. . . ."

Marcia's laugh rang out. Mockingly her voice followed it, "Information about Linda Condrick, Inspector?" She half turned, to look at Linda. Her voice mocked, high and triumphant, "Who *are* you, Linda Condrick?"

CHAPTER XVI

MARCIA was singing softly to herself when Rowena came into the room. She stopped, looking at the girl, smiling—grinning—at her.

She said, with a high-pitched giggle, "Are you a murderess, Rowena pet?"

Rowena said coldly, "It's not funny. Not even a little bit."

Marcia's grin changed to a scowl as she pulled off the silk kimono and moved to the bed, groaning as she pulled her injured leg under the sheets. "Oh no, you wouldn't think so, of course. I think you've always tried your damndest to like Linda, because she marrying Greg and you like him and then of course you've got nothing to worry about, have you, pet—two thousand pounds all to yourself. You're nicely set."

She leaned back on the pillows and said, "But that story! Oh, Di's right. First time in my life I've ever agreed with her about anything—it's a ridiculous story, and *none* of us were scared by it. You saw. . . ."

"Marcia," Rowena stood with her back to the door, "you were out there tonight. In the darkness. Near the billabong."

Marcia's hand had been reaching for the paper-backed love novel. It stopped. Her head jerked forward. "What are you babbling about?" she snapped.

"I think you were out there. Or downstairs. Somewhere. And you said you were in bed and . . ."

"I was, pet." It came softly.

" No. Because someone came upstairs after me. . . ."

" Linda."

" No. I've thought and thought and that wasn't Linda. When I came back first it was just like I told the police— I was scared out of my wits and my heart was thudding so much I don't believe I would even have heard an elephant coming up the stairs. But then I calmed a bit and it was then I heard soft steps coming up. And I looked out. It was all dark and then I heard Gregory downstairs—running and slamming doors and I looked towards the stairs and when I looked down the landing again whoever had been there was gone."

" Linda. Of course it was Linda."

" No," Rowena denied again. " I've thought and thought as I said and I'm sure it wasn't her. She must have come up right after me and been in her room by then because —if you stand by my door and look towards the stairs— Linda's room would be on your right. Yours is on the left. And no one passed me. They couldn't have. I would have felt them go by, seen their shadow in the darkness. It wasn't Linda's. Because no one passed me."

" She came this way, knowing that and then . . ."

" No. Because when I heard Greg I opened my door quite wide and stood there listening. And I remember that suddenly there was a line of light under Linda's door. So she was in there. And she couldn't have passed me. It was someone else who came up quietly like that and that means . . . where were you, Marcia? "

Marcia laughed.

" Pet, as a detective you're a frost. Mrs. Leeming's room is next to this, remember."

" I . . ."

" Mrs. Leeming, pet. She was probably downstairs getting herself a snack or something and saw you and Linda

156

pussy-footing upstairs. As for coming up softly. She'd do that as a matter of course so she wouldn't disturb anyone who was asleep."

Rowena turned, and opened the door. She looked back. She said, "And did she leave the stair light and the landing light off too to save disturbing someone, and walk in the dark? An old lady. . . ."

Marcia said nothing. Her brittle gold hair was fanned out on the pillow and the love novel was up, hiding her face.

For a long time lights danced near the billabong, circling, then centring together again, only to spread out once more. Rowena knelt by the window watching them. She knew what they were looking for—the rifle. One was missing from the house—one of Gregory's—and it was out there somewhere, tossed away when its job was done.

When Quince and Cherside had dismissed them and some way everyone was tucked under the homestead roof for the night, Linda had walked upstairs like a sleep-walker, feet hardly lifting with each step, one hand trailing flabbily over the banister, her gaze unseeing. Everyone had been on the landing to see her pass. Even Gregory, who had tried to stop her, to speak to her. She had ignored him, as she ignored them all and went with that sleep-walker's look into her room. They all heard the key turn in the lock.

Eyes had shifted. Gazes crossed. Question and answer had flowed back and forth silently along the landing as Gregory too had gone to his room without a word to any of them. Finally they had all moved, drifting apart, still with those glances, rising smiles, flowing gently back and forth, stirring thought and the slumbering satisfaction that lay beneath their silence.

On the ridge the rising northern wind was moving

silently and stirring the top layer of ash on the western end of the ridge on the margin where the fire had been turned back before the south wind, scattering it and stirring what lay below, whirling ash before it in ever-fining fragments of black and grey, filling the air above the ridge with them, letting them fall, tossing them up again, spreading them as finest dust over the ridge's scars, blowing it gently away down the ridge towards the valley, to uncover the smouldering hot redness of a fallen tree trunk.

In the margin between night and dawn a little runnel of fire went snaking in crazy rivulets across brief patches of dried green amongst the black of the previous fire's margin. Passing the far reaches of it the rivulets found new fuel on either side of them. They spread out, joining together to form one solid unbroken advancing front of fire.

By the time the police stood on the main homestead's verandah at seven in the morning the whole western end of the ridge was under a cloud of smoke and Hudson and Billy and Gregory were gone.

Quince said sharply, as Rowena met them with the news, "I told you none of you were to leave the valley."

She said simply, "They were needed. The fire got away and its nearly at the bottom of the ridge now."

He said crisply, the affableness, the consideration, gone from his voice, "The rest of you are not to leave under any circumstances."

She said gently, not looking at him, "If the fire races across the valley we'll have to get the sheep into the billabong to give them a chance and leave the dogs to hold them there while we all join the men."

Quince threw up his hands in exasperation, but said with sudden lightness, "And I suppose if worse becomes worst you'll tie a couple of tails to me and Cherside and use us as stand-ins for the dogs, too?"

She smiled and he said, " But no one is to leave. That's an order that is to be obeyed. Sergeant Gambell will request the women in Fobb's Creek to come over and give what help is needed to the firefighters—keep them supplied with food and render any first-aid necessary. Do you understand? "

" Yes," she agreed, but her eyes scorned, " But that's not to say we'll really obey."

She knew he had understood because for a moment there was that exasperation in his long lean face again; then he said shortly, " Now that you're here I want you to go over your memory of last night again."

He took her all through it—twice. Right down to where John Dolley had said, " I saw the two of them come down to the gully . . ." and the shot that had sent him bowing backwards, then forwards, and sent her fleeing back to the homestead.

She agreed, as she had done before, that she had thought the shot had come from a little to her right. No, she said, she hadn't seen anything of Linda. And no, she denied, no one else had been out to her knowledge. She had no intention of telling him of her talk with Marcia; of her question to Mrs. Leeming, " Were you downstairs tonight —when I came back? When Linda came back? And after did you come quietly upstairs—in the dark? " Mrs. Leeming had said aggressively, " If I had, wouldn't I have said? I saw nothing. And I did nothing but go to my bed, which is what you should have done yourself."

All that was something to be thought about quietly, in silence.

When he had finished she drew a long breath of relief, that finished in a little jerk of fright as he said, " Where is Linda Condrick? "

" I . . . in her room, I think. I haven't seen her this morning. Are you going . . ."

159

"Don't ask questions, Rowena," was all the satisfaction she got to that. "Please ask her to come downstairs to the living-room to me."

She wanted, as Diana had done before, to refuse. She didn't want to face Linda, but in the end she went inside without another word to him. And she saw them all. All watching. All waiting. All gazing at her and the men who walked behind. Diana, and Wilma and Mrs. Leeming from the hall doorway to the kitchen, and from the landing Marcia was watching, too.

Rowena went past them without speaking. Brushed past Marcia on the landing and went to knock on Linda's door.

She called, "It's Rowena, Linda. The police want you now. Downstairs."

The door opened at once. If Linda had remained awake in fear and anxiety during the night it didn't show on her face or in her eyes. She was dressed neatly in trim grey slacks and a white shirt, a yellow scarf at her throat and her dark hair was smooth, her mouth outlined in coral lipstick.

She went past without a word and didn't even seem to see Marcia. She went downstairs and said, "Good morning, Inspector," as though last night had never happened. Rowena, looking over the landing railing, saw her and the policeman go into the living-room and the door shut. The three in the kitchen doorway moved too. Into the kitchen, shutting the door. To put their heads immediately to the panels of the door to the living-room, Rowena was certain. And Marcia, holding tight to the banisters, stumped slowly, carefully, but eagerly down into the hall to place herself against the hall door, smiling mockingly up at Rowena.

It was horrible, yet Rowena herself fled to Ella's room and ducked under the mantelpiece, to kneel in the great chimney and listen too. The whole house was listening to the stranger within its doors.

She was saying, ". . . nothing to add."

Quince said, "I am waiting on a report from Sydney. I am telling you this because I want you to understand that your whole background is under complete investigation. Knowing that . . ."

Linda laughed.

The sound came floating clearly up the chimney.

Then Linda said, "And knowing that you expect me to start another statement . . . to—what did Diana call it?— to shift and turn, again. No, Inspector, I've not a word to add to what I said last night. Someone in this house tried to kill me. And when they didn't—when someone died instead—they have used everything they possibly could to make me suspected of Golden's death. They can never, never prove anything. But . . ."—suddenly her voice cracked—"they can make Gregory doubt me. That's what they're counting on now. Driving me out. And they'll never let him forget me—or what they'll call his mistake in ever getting engaged to me. Can't you see them? Always at him—to divide the valley—to give more and more as they waste what they already have! And if he refuses— they'll remind him of me and his mistake and the suffering it brought to me. To *them*."

Quince said quietly, "There's no need for dramatics, Miss Condrick."

There was silence. Rowena wondered what Linda's expression was then. When it seemed Quince wasn't going to believe her—when he was just waiting on a report before he told her to pack and go with him.

He was saying, "You are not to leave the homestead."

"Don't worry," she said tightly. "I'm not leaving. Unless

you arrest me. Or Gregory throws me out. Otherwise I'm staying."

She knows we're listening, Rowena thought. That was a challenge to us all. A defiant warning that she intends to win, if she can.

In spite of herself a faint warmth of admiration and something else touched her as she knelt there. Whatever Linda Condrick might be, she could fight.

Quince was asking, "Tell me again what happened when the shot came last night. You were squarely facing Dolley, so you told me."

"Yes. You must know that as you found my lighter. Gregory had his back to me."

"But you could still see Dolley's face."

"Oh yes," she agreed dryly, "I could see him. He was actually a perfect target for someone with a rifle. There was darkness all round him, and his face showing in the light of the camp-fire."

It was almost as though she no longer cared, as though she was showing him how easily she could have killed if she had needed to.

"You saw no one at all?"

"Only Gregory and John Dolley. I don't know where Rowena was—I saw nothing of her at all."

"She was on your left."

Her left, Rowena thought. Her left. And I've told him the shot came from my right!

"Dolley spoke . . . the shot came . . . and you dropped your lighter?"

"Yes," she answered in seeming impatience, "I've told you that a dozen times. He said something about seeing two people come down to the gully and on that word the shot crashed out. I was lighting a cigarette. I had my thumb on the lighter's flint actually, and I just dropped the

162

lighter from shock. I tried and tried to find it, but I had no light to see by and the ground was covered with leaves."

Quince said slowly, "I saw two of them come down to the gully . . . and then the shot. All right, that's all I want. Would you send Mrs. Leeming in to me? "

Mrs. Leeming said aggressively, "I've not a word more to tell either of you."

"Good," Quince said affably, "then you can repeat the ones you've already told us. Sit down."

She must have obeyed because he said next, "That's right. Now think back to last night. You went off to bed, didn't you? But funny things have been happening round here and there was a stranger by the billabong last night. I think you would have liked to have known the homestead was locked up nice and tight last night before you put your head on your pillow? "

She said nothing.

"I think you should have waited until everyone was upstairs and gone down to make sure. You're not the type to tell your fears to others. You would just have slipped down. If you'd stood by your window, waiting and listening, you would have seen, as Rowena Searle did, a light going towards the billabong? "

She still said nothing.

He suggested again, "And you might have gone downstairs to wait till whoever it was came back. You'd be curious to see who it was. So you'd sit in the dark, wouldn't you? "

There was still silence.

Quince said, "You were still dressed. And that big white apron would make a patch of lightness even in the dark. That was what Gregory Forst saw for a moment as he came in. That was why he didn't follow that person upstairs. He knew it was you. And he couldn't see you as the one by the billabong. But he told me about it."

She sniffed. "Well, what if I did want to see the place locked up? Oh, all right, you can stop wasting your breath and your brainpower in worrying over me. I came down and I sat there—in that chair right there."

"Well?"

"The windows were open. I heard that shot as clear as I hear you now. It frightened me. There was no need or reason for no shots at that time of night. Not even Dolley would be looking for rabbits for the pot. No, I was scared. And I waited. And then I saw them—Rowena and Miss Condrick. They just missed one another by a cat's whisker. Rowena whisked in and up. *She* followed. Neither of them stopping to put on lights. Didn't make sense. I waited again, and then I heard someone running. I was suddenly scared all through and I went for my life for the stairs."

"And that's all you can tell me? You never left the house yourself?"

"No. Never."

"You didn't see anything else moving out there?"

"No. Never."

"And Mrs. Forst—Mrs. Marcia Forst—was in her room?"

There was silence.

He repeated the question.

She said in sudden quavering fear, "No, she wasn't. Oh, I was that scared. Rowena was in her doorway. I could see it was a bit ajar. And I thought she'd see me move to my room—right down the landing. I went into Mrs. Forst's. There was no light under the door. If she'd been awake I could have said I'd heard noises—wondered if she was wanting anything. She wasn't there."

Quince said dryly, "I think you went in deliberately

just to see if one person in the place had really gone to bed that night or not? Well?"

"What if I did?"

"Nothing, except that your curiosity is proving a help to us. You run away and send Mrs. Forst in here."

Marcia giggled. She said, "Well, if you really want to embarrass me—I was in the bathroom. Sitting in state! Did you think I wanted to admit that when you asked? I'd been to bed and then I got up again. And there I was when the house seemed to practically explode. I popped out and there was Gregory banging on Rowena's door and saying, 'Come down. You're wanted,' and I slipped into my room without him seeing me. And don't you go telling me I've got to get up in some court and say that to the world or I'll pass out."

Quince said dryly, "If and when you stand up in court, Mrs. Forst, you'll be on oath—to tell the truth."

He doesn't believe her, Rowena thought. He's warning her that she's going to be asked again—on oath. She knelt there asking herself if, as she had stood there, her own door slightly ajar, there had been one stretch of light close to the landing floor—a sliver of it under the bathroom door, to prove Marcia's statement.

She said aloud, to the bricks of the huge chimney, "I didn't see a light at all."

She had to repeat that to Quince and Cherside. To his witness, she reminded herself tautly. Their faces were as blank of expression as the bricks of the chimney had been as she said, "I didn't see a light. I'm sorry, but I didn't. I can't say whether she was there or not. But the bathroom's on my side the landing. I was looking towards the stairs really. I mightn't have noticed a sliver of light on my side

165

the landing. And then Gregory made a terrible noise. If Marcia had just turned out the light she might have stood still, listening and wondering what on earth was going on."

"That's right," Quince agreed, "She might. We're going down to the billabong now. After all if you're intending to drive a mob of sheep into it I'm not going to pick up anything to help me later than this morning. Remember what I said about not leaving the house. Remember it until I come back."

Mick Gambell was in the house. He had come up as soon as Quince and Cherside had left. Rowena had tried to draw him into the kitchen but he had said gruffly, "I have to stay by the phone, Rowena. And by the way, the arrangements are all made. Some of the Fobb's Creek people will be helping the men."

"Stay by the phone!" Wilma had taunted when Rowena had reported to the others what Mick had said. "What he means is—stay where he can see the verandah, and the stairs and outside all at once. Where he can see if any of us dare leave. But it proves, you know, it's Linda they're going to take away." When Rowena had gazed at her blankly the elder girl had said impatiently, with a toss of her head that sent her thick brown hair flying, "If they believed her story they'd have an eye on Gregory and Hudson and dad as well as us. And they're not even worrying about them so far as I can see. No, it's Linda Condrick they're after."

From time to time the phone rang, bringing them all to the hall to watch and listen to Mick answering. Each time he answered curtly, put the phone back and shrugged at them, "Not important," and went back to staring towards the stairs as though he was expecting to see Linda Condrick appear on the landing. She had gone back to her room and

166

appeared to have no interest now in what was going on below.

Then suddenly there was a difference. Mick answered the phone yet again. And stiffened. His gaze flicked over them. He said shortly at last, "Rowena, run down to the billabong and ask the Inspector to come up. Sydney wants him. Hurry!"

Sydney, she thought, as she fled. Sydney! A report on Linda was coming through.

Quince saw her coming and strode to meet her. He looked angry and said, "I thought . . ."

"Mick sent me," she said breathlessly, "Sydney wants you. Do hurry!"

Surprisingly Quince made no effort to shoo away the avid faces and listening ears, but they couldn't hear what the caller was saying and Quince's answers were limited to, "Yes. I see. You're positive. All right, thanks very much. Yes, I'll let you know. Thanks."

He replaced the receiver. His gaze ran over them all. Then shifted towards the stairs. There was movement on the landing, the steps. They all turned. They were all gazing up at the girl who stood there as Quince asked softly, "Who *are* you, Linda Condrick?"

Rowena saw the jerk of her body as she stopped dead, staring down at him. "What . . ."

"Who *are* you, Linda Condrick?" he asked again. "What is your name? There's no record of any child of your name being made a ward of the State and being put in foster homes. There's no record of anyone of your name being born at all. Who are you, Linda Condrick?"

CHAPTER XVII

LINDA came down the stairs. She said, " I had no idea you'd go back so far. What on earth has my childhood, my very birth, got to do with you? "

" What is your real name? " Quince asked.

" Williamson," she said shortly.

" Why did you change it? "

" I . . . the reason is quite private. It can be no concern of yours at all. I do assure you that. . . ."

" I still want to know. Come on in here," he gestured her into the living-room and closed the door on the avid faces that watched greedily, hungrily.

Marcia laughed into Rowena's shocked eyes. Her hand went out and patted, with increasing force till it was almost savagely hitting the smooth skin, " What now, pet? You never expected that, did you? You . . ."

" Oh no! "

Rowena turned and fled blindly up the stairs. She flung open the door of Ella's room and ran to the huge chimney and ducked and knelt, her pulse pounding in her throat.

She heard Linda say angrily, ". . . quite private! "

" Nothing is private when murder's been done. Come along, Miss . . . Williamson. Or is it Mrs.? "

" Miss. I'm not married. I've never been married. I changed my name when I was sixteen for purely private reasons."

" Then tell me—here in private—what they were."

" Private! I can just imagine they're practically fighting at the doors this minute to listen! "

"What have you got against them knowing?"

There was sudden weariness in Linda's voice. She said flatly, "Nothing of course. Not really. It's only . . . it concerned me alone, but I suppose it doesn't matter. And of course I've got to tell you, because you're suspecting me all over again, aren't you? My parents—he was a clergyman and she was a muscian, believe it or not—died when I was a toddler. I had an aunt, but she wouldn't take me in. She couldn't be bothered. So I've no reason to think kindly of my real name, have I? Every time I thought of it, once I knew, I thought of her. It was hateful.

"I was too old for adoption, it seemed. Everyone wanted tiny babies, so they sent me to a foster home. Oh, I loved it!" There was wild longing in her voice, "She was a beautiful person—fat and jolly and she had four sons of her own. She used to call me her little daughter, and she told me once I was going to be her own little daughter too. They were going to adopt me. Her husband was wonderful, too. And their name was Condrick. I think the adoption papers had actually been drawn up and then she fell sick. Terribly sick. She had to go into hospital, and there was no one to look after the little boys or me either. I was taken away. I know Mr. Condrick was terribly upset. I didn't find out till I was in my teens that Mrs. Condrick died about twelve months later. I never saw any of them again anyway. I was taken away and sent to some other home. They didn't like me and no wonder. I think I screamed the place down from rage and grief. And once I knew even screaming wouldn't get me back to Mrs. Condrick I . . . I wouldn't let myself love any of the foster people after that. Or even like them. I wasn't going to be hurt again! They said I was sullen and none of them would keep me long. I don't blame them.

"Then when I was fourteen I was taken away from

school and sent out to work. I wanted to nurse even then, but of course I couldn't start at that age. I was put in a shop. I loathed it. And I was terribly, horribly jealous of the other girls with their talk of families. I turned sullen on them, refused to join in the talk. They thought I was stuck-up. Everything seemed to go wrong. When I was old enough to start nursing I thought—Well, no one's ever liked Linda Williamson, except Mrs. Condrick. But now I'm starting a new life. And I thought what about a new personality, too? A less sullen one. I thought of a new name might help and, of course, I thought of Condrick. I talked it all over with the matron of the hospital where I was going to train. She was a nice person and sympathetic and understanding, though actually I would never have told her but for the fact I had to get my birth certificate and I'd put myself down as Linda Condrick on the application. She agreed the change of name might be a good idea and sometimes when I took to the sulks afterwards she would sidle up and whisper to me, ' Oh, Nurse Williamson—can you tell me where Nurse Condrick is this morning? '

" That is, quite honestly, the whole story."

Rowena had hardly been conscious of being shuffled into a smaller space, of being cramped against the cold brick of the chimney. She had been hardly aware of Marcia's cloying scent in her nostrils.

Then Marcia giggled softly at her side. " She ought to write for the Sunday papers! Honest, did you ever hear such a sob tale in all your nelly? "

Rowena looked at her. She whispered, " Don't you believe it? '

Marcia laughed. " Of course not. And neither do you, either, so come off the innocent looks! "

Rowena said clearly, pushing her away, trying to get

back to the bedroom, "But I don't know if I believe you either—about last night."

Marcia's body pressed her back against the brick. Marcia's voice said, "You watch out, pet," and then she moved, was crossing the bedroom and was gone.

Quince was asking, quite pleasantly, "You understand, don't you, that every word of this story can be checked?"

"Yes."

"And that I'm going to check it?"

"Yes."

"And in the meantime you are not to leave this house?"

"Yes."

"Very well. You may go, Miss . . ." Quince hesitated, then asked, still pleasantly, "What is it to be? Condrick? Or Williamson? Or . . ."

Linda said quietly, "You can call me anything you like. It doesn't matter. In a few weeks I will be Mrs. Forst."

Mrs. Leeming said aggressively, "What is it this time? Or aren't I to do any cooking at all today?"

"Not evasions," Quince said affably, "You've already cooked up enough of them. You come and sit down over here."

She snapped, "I haven't done no evasions. I've told you the whole truth. Of everything you've asked me."

"Yes, you've told me the truth, but not all of it. You've left out things that could have helped me. Things about this family. You come and sit down. You've been fifty years in this house. You've seen Mrs. McGuire and Mr. Hudson Forst come here and you've seen them marry, and you've seen Wilma McGuire and young Gregory Forst born. You must have come here when Gregory Forst's father was a small boy. Didn't you?"

"Yes. But . . ."

"You must have been here when Mrs. Ella Forst's daughter was born—that was forty-five years ago, wasn't it? Ten years after her brother was born. She was born in this valley, wasn't she? "

Rowena, listening eagerly, could hear only silence. Then Quince said very softly, " Oh yes—Linda Condrick's birth certificate wasn't all I asked the Sydney police to look for, Mrs. Leeming. I remember asking you about the family— about all the relationships. You told the truth there, but evaded just the same. Mr. Luke went away, you said, and his wife remarried. You skirted the truth because it reflected on the family, didn't you? Mr. Luke didn't die as it sounded. He deserted his wife and children, didn't he? And you said of old Ella Forst's daughter that she went away too and died unmarried. You didn't add, as you you should have done, that, unmarried or not, Louisa Forst had a child."

Mrs. Leeming whispered, "I've prayed you wouldn't find out and then I started praying you would. I didn't know what to do. And I couldn't be sure. I could only wonder if all I suspected and feared was right or wrong. Just so much nonsense or terrible wickedness. I can't get at what made you. . . ."

"But Louisa's child looks rather like Ella Forst, doesn't she? I saw the old lady's photos and I saw her features and the family eyes where they shouldn't have been at all." Quince's voice was surprisingly gently. "You're the only one who knew Ella Forst when she was young. Even when Diana and Hudson Forst came here Ella Forst must have been about fifty. None of them, except yourself, saw her as a young woman. But even in the photos I've seen of her in the house—all fairly recent ones taken by Rowena, so she told me—there's that likeness showing through."

172

Mrs. Leeming said wearily, "Oh, there's a likeness. They'd have known, I expect, ten or twenty years ahead. But . . . yes, there's likeness. Not the colour of hair, mind, but . . ."

"You knew definitely? Or just guessed?"

Rowena, even kneeling, could see across the room to that photograph of Ella. The level dark glance seemed to be peering at her; the dark features mocking; the arrogantly pointed chin held high. She went on staring at it, fascinated, as Mrs. Leeming's voice floated up the body of the chimney between the cold bricks.

"There was hardly any time I didn't guess. And I'd seen the father too, mind. A huge fellow. Dark as night, and huge. Louisa just set eyes on him and she went mad. They've all been like that. Diana with McGuire—he was a fool from the start, but he just walked in and she handed herself over without a word. And Hudson, too with Marcia. And Gregory . . . all of them the same. One look and they'd give the world if they had it to throw away. Louisa knew he was married. That was the badness of it. There were terrible scenes for a time and then she packed and went and it was like she was dead in the house. You weren't allowed to speak of her—not her own brother, nor Hudson nor Diana. I think they've about forgotten her completely now. And then a letter came. From him. Laughing at them. Telling old Gregory and Ella that they needn't worry about the shame of it any more because she was dead and buried."

"Wasn't there any word said about a child?"

"Never a word to me."

"You said you guessed, but you were also sure. . . ."

"That's right. After a time I couldn't bear not really knowing and just wondering and I wrote to a friend in Sydney and asked her to go to the registrar's and try to find out if there was a Louisa Forst what had had a baby and her not married, and I got the answer back. I never let on I knew, not even when the row came. If it'd come before it would have saved me writing that letter, because I heard it all come out then."

"The cat got out of the bag?" he said softly.

"Cat?" Her voice quavered up in mockery. "It was a full grown tiger that jumped on old Ella that day. I heard the yelling—'You old devil! You wouldn't let me have my rights! You wouldn't acknowledge me all these years either, because you wouldn't acknowldge a Forst could have a baby when she wasn't married! Well, I'm going to have my share of the valley. . . .' It went on and on. They were yelling till I thought the roof'd fly off with it and then afterwards . . . I was scared out of my wits. I knew whose child I was seeing then all right. I'd seen that look on *his* face once—the father's face. He'd quarrelled with old Gregory and been ordered to get right out of the district. He got a gun and he went round the valley shooting every beast he could find."

"But you said nothing to the others? And Mrs. Forst didn't either?"

"She was dead next day. Dead in the night. Or she might've, knowing what a devil she had loose in the place. And no, I said nothing. I didn't want any part of it. Let them all fight it out themselves, so I thought. But then Golden died. Accident, I said at first, and then you came and reckoned different and I started to worry. When nothing was said to the others to tell them they had another cousin I wondered what was happening . . . but just staying silent was no proof of having a hand in it." She said heavily, "It's on your shoulders now. You know, and I can't do a thing, can I?"

"No. Except answer a few more questions. About last

174

night, about Golden's death and Mrs. Forst's. About Louisa Forst. . . ."

The name seemed to echo in old Ella's bedroom. Louisa, the curtains seemed to rust. Louisa. . . .

The house seemed strangely silent in spite of the voices downstairs, in spite of the rustling of the curtains in the rising wind. Then noise was all through it like a whirl-wind. Doors crashed open and voices called and Mick's voice thundered up the chimney to Rowena, still crouched, listening.

"Fire's through. The message just came. It's coming straight across the valley."

Rowena staggered to her feet, seeing the curtains billow into the room with the rush of wind. She stared at them in horror. If a wind like that was carrying the fire ahead of it they were in serious trouble. She stood there a moment listening to the noises in the house, the pounding footsteps, the calling voices. She could see from the window, feel the wind on her face. Then she saw Mick, running from the house. And, in front of him, Linda.

Rowena slipped from the room. The hall was deserted and she ran down and out through the main doors. Linda and Mick were heading towards the little blue car. Some-time during the morning Linda must have parked it there outside the homestead. Rowena called to them, but they didn't look back. They went on running.

There was a cloud forming over the western end of the valley. To Rowena it looked as though a vast mob of sheep were being driven at an incredible speed across the valley, the dust of their flying progress billowing out before, behind and on either side of them. Then suddenly the cloud parted and she saw fire. It was leaping in orange-red strides up one tree, then a branch was falling, a bridge of fire that plummeted into the top branches of another tree and turned it to a pillar of flame in the time it took Rowena to turn her head. The whole valley seemed burning as out of the fringes of the cloud came frantic men, staggering, coughing, not fighting the unfightable now, but simply running.

Quince and Cherside saw it, too, and the station wagon stopped. The two stared in fascination at the little blue car bucketing across the floor of the valley. Neither men had spoken since those frantic five minutes when Mick Gambell had fled his post in the hall and run, and Quince had seen the blue car start up; heard it go.

Cherside had jumped for the phone, dialled and let it fall as he had seen the cut wires. Quince was by his side then, saying, "Where on earth's it heading?" and Cherside had answered greyly, "West. The fire'll close behind the car and we can't phone to the police that way or anywhere else."

Quince had snapped to the circle of white faces, "One of you get to the other homesteads—the nearest. Try to reach town . . ." and had taken Cherside and the station wagon and gone in pursuit, in silence.

Now, as the station wagon stopped and Cherside half rose in his seat, and they stared, Quince snapped, "Turn. We can't go on. Pick up some of those men and then run."

"But . . . look!" Cherside was pointing.

The car was running through the smoke, then slewed round almost to face the other way. Cherside said, "Something's gone. Steering probably . . ." and was silent again. Staring. As they were all staring. Black-faced, grimy men pausing in flight; policemen in the stopped wagon; and Rowena—all staring at the little blue car that was running crazily, out of all control, into the orange-red fire.

CHAPTER XVIII

THE curtains in old Ella Forst's bedroom were stirring gently, making hardly a whisper of sound. They no longer whispered loudly, "Louisa" as they had done the previous morning, but voices were coming up the chimney just as they had done before the blue car's flight. And though it was all over, it was easier to listen there and not to have to look at faces and see strained expressions and tired eyes.

Quince's voice came clearly into Ella's bedroom, "I was to blame. I told Mick Gambell to stay in the hall and not move out of it and report anyone moving around outside, but nothing more. I wanted him to hear what was being said, but I made a bad mistake. I should have kept him with me to take notes and left Cherside outside, but I'd forgotten the fire and the confusion that might result if it got through."

There was a little silence. She wriggled closer to the cold brick of the chimney, wishing now she could see them after all. Then Quince was going on, "But now there can be no trial—no imprisonment. It will make things a lot easier for the family. There'll be the inquests of course, but then it will be over, and the family will break up and scatter. Or have you changed your mind?"

Gregory said, "No. It would be too difficult for all of us to act normally after all the rows and backbiting and demanding. Anyway my grandmother was right. She left me a letter—the one I showed you—the one I would have showed them all if I hadn't been stunned by their reaction to the will. She said she knew she had ruined them by keeping them here and never letting them find their own feet. With money always for the asking they hadn't needed ambition, anything but an outstretched hand. She knew they didn't have any affection for her, either. And the money was all gone. I don't think she'd ever stopped to look ahead —they asked and she was so worried and grief-stricken over them she gave. I was going to pay Rowena's allowance from my own money. I couldn't have done anything else, because even to pay the death duties will force me to raise every penny I can on Leumeah, I'm afraid. It's going to take years to work off the debt. Diana has a bit put away —she could start a small business and perhaps Billy, with nothing more for the asking, will try to help. And Hudson —oh, he can work, but with money for the asking, just like Billy, he went to pieces—he was always gone on some holiday when we really needed him. With a job he has to stick to I think he'll manage. And I can't afford to keep them."

"You know," Quince said considerately, "I think young Mrs. Forst will pull her weight. After all she's kept him contented enough with her to stand four years of marriage. And talking of Marcia Forst—she was speaking the truth about the night Dolley died, though at the time I had my doubts. She actually was in the bathroom, but looking at her knee and trying to ease the pain of it. I saw it later and it was really nasty looking. She refused, so she tells me, to call a doctor because Linda hadn't considered it worth looking at and "—he sounded a little amused—" she wasn't going to have Linda Condrick looking down her nose in contempt. A matter of pride, so she told me. And that, you know, was one thing that interested me very much. Why did Linda Condrick, the trained nurse in the house, stand aside and ignore the woman who'd been brought back on a stretcher? She never even looked at her knee, let alone touched it. She left that to Rowena." And then he really did laugh outright. "And I've never before known a nurse who could resist taking over for even the simplest injury."

Linda's voice held a touch of laughter too as he admitted, "You're right." Then she added gravely, "I just couldn't have touched her to save my life. I kept looking at her and wondering if she were the one who'd tried to kill me. I just couldn't have touched her."

"I guessed that. It was one reason I believed in your story. One reason I threatened you with arrest to break your —silence—to get hold of that story."

"You guessed by then that . . . ?" her voice went up in astonishment.

"Oh yes. When I told you all the cyanide came from here and that only the women had known Golden went to the ridge, why didn't you realise that not one single one of you could have known that Golden went right to the top and remained there? Right from the beginning I was asking if Golden hadn't died in place of someone else. And once I thought of that I looked around and what did I see under my nose? Someone who was hated. Linda Condrick. Someone who was to be given the whole valley in a settlement to beat any further death duties on the estate in case Gregory Forst died in the next decade or so."

Linda said dryly, "None of them believed the reason was simply that. They all thought I'd some way dragooned Greg into agreeing to that. As though he was a piece of putty!" her voice scorned.

Quince asked, "You wouldn't like a husband like that?"

"I'd loathe it."

Quince said, "Oh, well, there was your packed case speaking for you too. You went up right after Golden. You

had no time to pack in panic when he first appeared—
you went straight to the ridge. And when you came down,
why pack if Golden had been a threat to you and the threat
was now dealt with? If you'd meant his death to look
natural there was no need to run. If you thought it would
appear to be murder, flight would be disaster, unless Golden
would be so easily connected with you we'd arrest you at
once. And in that case, why not fly at once? Why murder
at all? If killing meant leaving this valley and the man
who wanted to marry you it didn't seem to be going to get
you much.

"And then you packed those jewels. You weren't a pro-
fessional crook. You would have had no way of disposing
of the jewels. You were an intelligent woman and must
have realised that. Why take them? Of course you might
have been in such a state you didn't realise what you were
doing, but it looked as though it was innocent flight—a
flight with your possessions as the new mistress here.

"They were terribly small pointers to your innocence,
of course. And then came news from Sydney that you
weren't Linda Condrick at all. I admit that really shocked
me for a minute. I hadn't been searching that far into
your background at all. I'd asked Sydney to look up
Louisa Forst and they looked up everyone in a excess of
zeal. But it helped in a way. When it came out I'd looked
up your birth certificate, or lack of it, I saw another face.
Eyes wondering in panic who else had been looked up—
Rowena's." Wilma, in the room upstairs, winced at the
memory of the young girl the name evoked. "Oh, Miss
Rowena Forst saw the writing on the wall then. She saw it
more when I deliberately let her hear my talk with Mrs.
Leeming. I wanted to frighten her before I finally talked
to her. And I never allowed for that fire and Mick Gambell
being a bushman first and policeman second and deserting

his post. I didn't want to tell him the truth—he was too closely involved with the family altogether.

"I let Rowena hear that point that no one could have known where Golden was—which pointed to the truth of your story. And then I commented on Mrs. Leeming's evidence of when Dolley died. She saw you, Miss Condrick, and Rowena come back—almost together. Yet you, on your evidence, were hunting for your lighter. What was Rowena doing during that time? She knew you were there and where you were—I bet you walked down smoking and went to light another cigarette just as the shot came. She wanted you down there, you know—she threw at you the suggestion it was suspicious Dolley should by-pass the town. She told you Gregory was going to talk to him. It would have been odd if you, so closely involved, didn't watch Gregory and follow him.

"Right from the start Rowena interested me. She met us with a little girl look and seemed fearful, which might have been because of Mrs. Leeming's hissing remark that it was odd there were two of us.

"To put her at ease I informed her there had to be two, so one could be a witness to what the first claimed had been done or spoken at a given time. Her reaction could only be called peculiar. From then on she was continually gazing at Cherside as though she was asking, 'Are you witnessing this?' Once or twice when she was giving evidence or others were talking I thought she was actually going to yell at him, 'Get a move on, you fool, and get out your notebook and record this!'

"To go back to that first meeting though—the little girl look remained while in the brightest manner imaginable she took over the reins of the interview. We were far too slow getting down to bedrock for her. In those first few minutes she merrily informed us Linda Condrick was on the ridge when Golden died; Linda Condrick knew where cyanide was; Linda Condrick as a nurse would know it was poison; Linda Condrick had plenty of chances to talk to Golden privately when he was here before.

"From there on she continued her merry way of throwing suspicion on Linda. Never directly. Always indirectly. A phrase here . . . a look there, of doubt or fear or suspicion. And why all that and apparent holding-back of things, even before Golden's death was proved murder? Everyone else hardly noticed the police. They were quarrelling, showing their dislike of you completely and generally acting normally. Not Rowena. And, while she talked brightly of the money coming to her and how she had no reason to dislike Linda Condrick, her very actions showed a quite remarkable degree of hate. And not on account of the family. She despised them.

"She said she owed her settlement partly to Linda. She'd overheard Linda and you, Mr. Forst, discussing it. If you'd discussed that settlement, wasn't it possible you had also at the same time discussed giving the valley to Linda and giving her that jewellery?"

"Of course I did. The whole lot together."

"But still there was no apparent reason for her to worry about it. Until I saw a pointed chin. Small features. The same as in photographs of old Ella upstairs. Though Ella had auburn hair, Mrs. Leeming tells me. But I saw the family dark eyes, too. Oh yes, dark eyes are common and if you think carefully you'll realise that with people close to you every day you never really look at their eyes. But as a stranger, I did. It struck me as interesting.

"So did something else. McGuire told me bluntly that old Ella was mean to everyone outside her family. Why the considerable charity to Rowena Searle—a charity that went so far as asking her grandson to provide for the girl, while he was not asked to do so for Ella's family? It could, of course, have been because Rowena was much younger. Still. . . .

"But I still couldn't see, if Rowena really was a Forst, how she could know. She'd come here as a baby, and I couldn't see Mrs. Forst letting it out. Then Miss Condrick told me."

"*I* did," Linda jerked sharply.

"When you told us of a changing your name you said you had to tell the hospital matron because you'd made the application out in one name and you'd had to get your birth certificate which showed another. There it was—Rowena about to start her own training. The hospital she was going to must have asked for her birth certificate and then the cat . . . or as Mrs. Leeming says . . . the full grown tiger . . . was out of the bag and raging.

"According to Mrs. Leeming, Rowena went to Mrs. Forst that day the old lady died, while Linda was out walking, and told her what she knew. She demanded what she called her rights and the old lady told her she wasn't getting anything except perhaps a small allowance if Gregory provided it.

Linda said sharply, "Mrs. Forst . . . did . . ."

"Natural death. I'm certain of that. It was to Rowena's advantage to keep the old lady alive, work on her and apologise for that row and try to soften her in the future. But Mrs. Forst died and everyone was cut off with nothing.

"So there it was. Rowena wasn't legally entitled to anything. I think her first idea must have been to so stir up the family against Linda that she'd finally give up and go, when Rowena would suddenly discover her real identity and join with the family in demands on you, Mr. Forst. She must have known the family wouldn't help her unless they got something themselves—the family motto," he said dryly, and in the bedroom Wilma winced again, "seems to be 'a share for me or none for you'."

"Then she heard that discussion about her own future; about Linda getting the whole valley; and the jewellery into the bargain, and the tiger jumped out of the bag again.

"You all treated her as a child, but she wasn't and underneath you knew it yourselves, or why did you let her sit in on family rows? She was between child and woman and flew from one extreme to the other.

"That brooch was childish. It stood out a mile. Would someone whose living depended on a decent reputation steal something when she'd be the first suspected? Even more, would she steal when she was on the verge of getting a place here as mistress of the house? And Rowena was so busy casting suspicion on you that she happily agreed the others didn't know about the will which made you a liar in your reasons for keeping quiet about the brooch. However, if you were believed it meant no one had a reason for getting rid of you then. If they thought the valley was to be shared out they wouldn't have cared if you'd married a Hottentot, Mr. Forst.

"That left a piece of sheer spite and next I learned Miss Rowena had had her ears boxed for sticky-beaking in what didn't concern her. . . ."

Linda said, "I was ashamed afterwards, but I was horrified at the way the others continually used her to spy on each other. That was one reason I was so glad she was leaving. I told her she was well rid of the family, not realising. . . ."

"No, you weren't to realise a lot of things," Quince rejoined. "That she'd told an apparently senseless lie about seeing you, for instance. She said she stood at the western end of the gully and watched you rush down. When we went up, burned trees hid the view of the gully unless you stood in full view, and that afternoon the trees weren't burned at all. All those leafy branches would have hidden the gully altogether. She would have had to have stood smack in the end of the gully herself, if her story was true. You'd have seen her. Why the lie? "

Linda said slowly, "It was her coming out with that that made me dismiss her from any suspicion even if I'd thought . . oh, she *did* seem such a child! "

"She was careful, when she wanted, to make that impression. Stuck her thumb in her mouth and looked innocent. And remember she was the one who knew you were due to leave the ridge. She'd probably been following you most of the day trying to get you alone. She wouldn't have cared if your body hadn't burned and it was called murder. She didn't have any reason for murdering poor Linda, did she? But all the others hated her. Plenty of suspects around."

"Oh, she wouldn't have. . . ."

Quince's voice hardened, "Don't you go deluding yourself, Miss Condrick. She would have. When it looked as though you might get a bit of belief she was quite willing to let suspicion slide towards Marcia Forst. She wouldn't say if Marcia had been in the bathroom or not, though I'm certain she knew she had. She was always thinking ahead, wondering if she'd say this . . . or perhaps that and throw suspicion; also, too, thinking of simple unsuspicious reasons for her own actions. I bet she opened that case of yours for instance just to see if you'd packed that jewellery —and she got a shock!—but she told everyone she was doing her good girl's deed for the day and had wanted to unpack for you.

"And why didn't she tackle you immediately about the brooch? Why wait so long—until the police were there and would be sure to learn about the resultant explosion?

"But we couldn't go to court and talk of the way she acted—we couldn't speak of asking her about the brooch and seeing her start to shake and wondering if the look in her eyes wasn't excitement. It certainly wasn't fear. We couldn't talk of her odd actions in the way she cast suspicion—that very day she let out about seeing you on the gully she didn't do it openly. She told Wilma McGuire. Standing where she could see into the hall mirror downstairs and see me in the living-room doorway. We couldn't go to court and have Cherside tell of hearing her promise you, Mr. Forst, that 'I'll look after Linda'. Cherside says if you'd seen her eyes then, Mr. Forst, you'd have done some wondering. She meant what she promised, all right, but not the way you thought she did."

Linda said shakily, "She was mad. She couldn't be responsible for . . ."

Quince said shortly, "Don't start wasting pity. This is something else for you to think over. Mrs. Leeming says that during that fight old Mrs. Forst said, 'You've have your share of the valley and more. I've given you a decent home and I had to pay your father a fortune to get you in the first place. That was your share of Leumeah.' It was a pity she didn't . . . or didn't want to . . . believe it."

Linda pleaded, "Please don't . . ."

"All right—we'll turn to something else. Dolley. He wasn't the type to tackle a murderer. But he saw something that surprised him. There was what he said—'I saw two of them'. Both you and Mr. Forst used that phrase. Rowena said, 'I saw *the* two of them', a far different thing that meant Golden and someone else. But two of them meant two people of the same type—not a swaggie and someone else. Two firefighters, or two women, or two people from Leumeah. It could be any of them. I think Golden was dead when Dolley woke up. He saw you, Miss Condrick,

186

jump down and turn Golden over and then go for your life. And straight afterwards Rowena must have come running to see what on earth had happened. Dolley saw two women. He almost certainly went to gaze at Golden himself and probably thought he'd had a heart attack and help was on the way so he simply cleared out. But when the story hit the district he must have puzzled over the two of you who'd remained silent.

"Rowena, you know, must have spent a terrible time wondering what you intended to do, Miss Condrick."

Wilma could hear the scuffle of chairs from downstairs. Then Quince said, "I doubt if she'd have got away even if the steering of the car hadn't gone haywire."

Linda said shortly, "I knew it wasn't safe. Wilma used it the night of the fire and told me. I forgot about it, then remembered this morning. I was trying to keep my mind on other things and I rang the Fobb's Creek garage and asked a mechanic to come out, and parked the car out front."

"Without saying a word to her? But after she was thrown out when the car slewed round she couldn't have lived for more than a few minutes—just time enough, I expect, for her to see the car going running into the flames all by itself."

His voice was fading, and steps were getting fainter, as though everyone was moving towards the door. Wilma strained to hear. Heard only a mumble. Then a voice asked right behind her, "Why didn't you come down?"

Wilma pulled herself upright, her cheeks red. She said, "I couldn't, Mick. How could I face Linda? None of us can. I'm glad we're going. Oh, Mick, we're a dreadful family! There's a bad streak in us all right. . . ."

"Or maybe in some of the people you marry. Rowena was her father all over again if you ask me." Mick stood

187

looking at the photograph of Ella Forst, then he said, in a too casual tone, "and if you want to know, my great-grandfather first came out because he was deported for stealing."

Wilma started to laugh. She went on and on till his big hands took her shoulders and started to shake her. He said softly, "Is there a bad streak in you, Wilma? There's not in your mother. Oh yes, she acted badly, but people afraid never act normally. And nearly everything she took from old Ella was given to Billy and used-for you. Wasn't it?"

"Yes. And it's true you know—the money always being there for the asking ruined us. Dad got lost in dreams . . . but now we're going."

"And what about Gregory Forst? And yourself?"

She shook her head. "I was furious with him when he told me he wouldn't marry me. I wanted him back. And mother and dad kept urging me to *get* him back, but . . ."

He said, "Come on downstairs. I want to talk to you. We're going to do a lot of talking between now and when your family goes. And perhaps . . . you won't be moving far. Would you mind that? Would Gregory and Linda mind?"

She didn't say anything. And neither of them went down, for a long time.

Gregory and Linda were walking slowly over the valley. The whole western half of it lay like a dark blot of evil, spread downwards from the darkness of the ridge. They'd defeated the fire with the break against the valley and with water desperately pumped from the billabong, and with the luck of the wind dying to nothing. They'd fought and they'd won half of it. That was something.

Gregory said, "The fire's going to make it even harder

to get back on our feet. We'll have a debt over our heads for donkey's years. And ghosts." He turned to look at her. "Are you afraid of ghosts, Linda?"

"I don't think so. I don't think I'll ever be afraid of anything again. I've defeated fire—and if you'd asked me months ago if I could ever have stood in front of a raging fire and helped beat it back I'd simply have run! I've defeated hate and suspicion and all sorts of fears; and self-disgust at the way I ran in the first place and . . . oh, dozens of things, including the possibility of losing you.

"And I've learned not to be so intolerant. It was a lesson I badly needed I think, but . . . I despised them. She was so old and so tired and she knew they were just beggars and didn't have one scrap of affection for her."

She was silent, standing there with her arm linked in his. Then she said, "And I've learned not to be afraid of myself. The day I came here I looked round the valley and the house and I knew I wanted them both. Think what you like of that, Gregory Forst. And I wanted you, too. I'd promised myself I'd never love anyone or anything and get hurt again and then all in one day I'd given my whole soul to a valley and to you. I was horrified. And scared. I'm not any more."

She looked again at the dark shadow that had taken half of the valley. It was horrible. Trees, grass, fences, everything that had lived in the west had gone, right down to the very ants that had made its earth their own.

Gregory said, "Wait till Spring. There'll be new grass and I've hopes some of the trees will come to life again. Some of them will be burnt out of course, but others. . . ."

She smiled, that dazzling smile that lit and changed her whole face. She said, "And you'll work like a galley slave and I'll work to help pay the bills. You know this would be an ideal place for invalids—the climate's quite good and it's beautiful and I'm a nurse. And you needn't look like that. Remember that debt hanging over our heads! We'll make out someway though."

Deliberately she turned her back on the ridge; on the dark shadow over half the valley. He had to turn with her. She walked with him back into the sunlight and stopped. They were looking at the homestead, at the billabong, at the sheep that looked like story-book ones in the fading daylight. She remembered another evening and other people who had turned their backs on disaster. Her shoulders straightened and her head went back. She said, looking carefully ahead, "Pretty, isn't it?" and her voice was warm with content.